Copyright © 2021 by Jan Foster

Published by So Simple Published Media
First edition February 2021

Cover Design
© J. L. Wilson Designs | https://jlwilsondesigns.com

Paperback ISBN-13: 978-1-9163408-6-2
E-Book ISBN-13: 978-1-9163408-3-1

www.escapeintoatale.com

Risking Destiny

CHAPTER 1 – LANDING

The red-hued sails appeared through the mists just before dawn. Their colour should have heralded a warning to the labouring crews aboard the fishing boats, but they barely had time to tack around and try to head back to Pierowall before being subjected to a barrage of arrows and spears. Shouts of encouragement in a strange guttural language were the last sounds they heard. Sleek curved prows with carved dragon heads overtook the smaller vessels as the fishermen bled into their nets.

By the time the springtime sun had risen above the rooftops of the ground-hugging dwellings, it was too late to rally. Too late to locate weapons, too late to don shoes and certainly too late to find pails of water to douse the fires which quickly spread through the haystacks. The elders could only watch in horror as leather-clad giants dragged their children and women out of their stone sanctuaries. Then, they themselves were hustled down the tight passages between homesteads, laughed at if they tripped or slipped on the muddy pathway.

Resistance was met with swords, unmercifully driven through the torso as the screams of submission came too late. Commands the Orkneans didn't understand urged them, with arm gestures and shouts, towards the beach-head. Shivering from wind and fear, the remaining villagers were poked into a line, forced to their knees at the point of an enormous blade, and kicked if they complained.

The sun had barely crept above the trees in the distance beyond the village, and the conquest was complete. Seagulls squawked overhead, daring each other to dive down and strut before the defeated, mocking them with their freedom.

"They don't look strong enough to pull an oar," laughed Sigurd, looking over at his older brother with a gleeful victory smile. "This one is so old, he served at Thor's birth!"

The elder in front of him shivered as tears ran down his wrinkled face, but he kept his head held high and stared defiantly at the dread-locked conqueror before him. Sigurd had to admire his attitude, although he knew his brother would make a judgement about the man's future based more on his physique and age. He wasn't a cruel man, but all Northmen understood feeding mouths took effort. It had to be worth it.

Rognval, greying yet still strong and towering over the captives, grunted as he began examining the islanders. One woman spat on his boots as he walked down the line; she received a swift blow to the head from Torv standing behind her and fell, face first, quietly into the sand. Next, her son screamed and jumped to his feet, rushing at the broad chest blocking the sunlight in a futile defence of his mother. Rognval merely caught his tousled brown hair and held him at arm's length. The lad, maybe no more than ten years old, was half his height, but he lashed towards the Yarl with clawed hands and legs flailing, kicking.

"They have spirit though," Rognval muttered, his attention

once more turning to the assembled villagers. "How many menfolk are left?" He sneered at the boy and shook the lad by his head as he lifted him clear from the ground. "How many?"

Screaming from being held aloft by his scalp, the boy couldn't answer - he didn't know what the giant was asking. Even if he had understood, he wouldn't have known the right counting words. Sigurd winced.

Rognval released his hand, and the boy dropped to the sand. Torn with indecision, the skinny child chose to crawl over to his mother's body rather than fight again.

"There must be fifteen or so here, and probably another few back at the buildings who didn't want to join us on the beach," Sigurd said. Behind him, the flames had dwindled, replaced by columns of grey smoke rising into the air briefly before being dispersed by the wind. "I'll secure these if you want to look at the village?" He breathed in the scent of their devastation; the ash caught in the back of his throat with a bitter taste. The surge of energy he depended on during the brief fight was waning, and now they had to face their conflicting emotions and make the hard decisions.

Rognval nodded briefly, "Ivar will need the men back at home, the women can be roped ready to sail with them. Kill the oldest ones, they never sell for much and cost more to feed than they fetch." The boy would count as a man - crossing the sea, manning the oars, would tire the fight out of him soon enough.

Rognval sheathed Breath-Slayer and headed towards the village. Crossing a field, not far away from the shores where he had waited whilst his men rampaged, he plodded up the well-worn path. Sigurd watched his brother's shoulders slump as he leaned into the wind. Yarl Rognval the Fearless was getting too tired for fighting, although it pained Sigurd to even think so. This was supposed to be his brother's last and greatest adventure but, Sigurd thought his kinsman, his rock, might be losing enthusiasm for the blood spilling part of conquest.

Pausing to survey the flat landscape, Rognval bent down and picked up a clump of the soil. He crumbled it and sniffed the remnants - despite its dark sandy texture, he was checking whether the earth here was more fertile than home. Sigurd suspected his brother was already planning ahead. An experienced leader of raids, he would probably send one of the ships back with the slaves. Depending on the spoils they found here, their other two boats would continue onward to find more. It was possible some young warriors would want to return, to settle on the territory now they had claimed it. But for Rognval, only gold seemed of interest; he spoke more these days of funding his son's future victories.

Sigurd kept a stern face as he watched the crew tie up the villagers. Once they were secure, he left to explore. Taking the same path as Rognval, he reflected on their easy victory. Thor would have no warriors to welcome at his table today. It didn't matter to Him how quickly the battle had been won; it only counted that a Northman died with courage. However, after all the anticipation and gathering of men to follow the brothers in discovery, it nevertheless seemed anticlimactic to walk so easily into an unknown land with no Norse lives lost.

Still, it left more warriors for the next fight.

Ahead lay the cluster of low-roofed buildings which had appeared barely visible from the sea as they neared, looking instead like one large rock in the landscape. If it hadn't been for the fishermen, taken unawares by their approach as they launched their nets just a mile or so from shore, how easily they could have missed their target. How simple it had then been to spot the smoke drifting upwards as they skirted the edges of these islands, and row against the tide to land.

He caught up with Rognval looking around the fenced field in front of the dwelling complex. Low rising thatched roofs sat on top of thin curved walls, clustered together as if there wasn't enough space to be separated. In between the rooftops, what looked like slate-covered corridors connected the dwellings. Sigurd realised that the houses must be built partially into the landscape, otherwise there wouldn't be room to stand up inside. A small flock of sheep and goats corralled in one corner of the area bleated their distress as they witnessed more of their masters' murderers approach.

The brothers counted seven bodies strewn amongst the livestock, hacked down as they sought to flee. Most were only wearing a long brown shirt, their slumbers disturbed by the Northmen's arrival. A few had attempted to tie a woollen kilt into a skirt around themselves, before facing their attackers. Unfortunately, the stretch of material had provided little protection, and for one - his feet entangled in the fabric where he fell - it had been more of a hindrance.

Arvan emerged, blinking in the sunlight. His face was still decorated with blood, long red hair hid the splatters better.

Rognval frowned as he peered down the steps leading into the almost subterranean houses.

"No gold yet, Lord," Arvan muttered his disappointment.

Rognval clapped him on the back as Arvan stood aside to let them squeeze past. "Odin was beside you today," Rognval acknowledged Arvan's leading role in the attack.

"A reward in Valhalla isn't what I came for," he grumbled. "Barely worth sharpening Soul-Wrecker for!"

Rognval's huge frame filled the narrow passage, and he had to duck to enter the low doorway of the first chamber. Following him in, Sigurd hastily let loose his breath as the smell of close living assaulted his nostrils. After voyaging at sea for some weeks, he had forgotten the rank stench of bodies and animals packed into a small area. As his eyesight adjusted to the gloom, he realised that this was just one of a network of cramped rooms, connected by the dark stone covered passages.

"Why do they have to live so closely when they have all this space?" Sigurd wondered aloud, his innate curiosity overtaking his disgust.

"Wind," Rognval replied. "She must gust over this island like Thor's breath." Using his sword, Rognval prodded the blankets pushed in haste to the rush-strewn floor. Baskets and hide bundles had already been emptied, pulled from recessed shelves along the sides and strewn across the floor in the hunt. Treasured winter stores, dried meats and wooden tools - no hint of a metallic glint though.

Having poked through the ashes of the fire in the centre of the room, neatly contained within a square stone surround,

Sigurd knelt down next to the low ledges running around the walls. As he pushed his sword through mattresses of straw beds, he suppressed a shudder. The scattered stalks yielded nothing today, but, he had found hidden treasures in stranger places before.

His cheeks flushed, and not just from the retained warmth of trapped heat in the stone walls. How confined the dwelling was - completely different from their wooden lofty longhouses. To him, the enclosed rooms were a prison. They hadn't allowed the villagers space enough to escape either. Just the bulk of the brothers' torsos, thick with muscles and fur, crowded the tiny room. Their eyes met, and Rognval grunted his displeasure. Turning to leave, Rognval kicked the pots aside as he ducked his head on his way out.

Alone, Sigurd felt a pang of guilt. He could appreciate how these small family dwellings afforded privacy and security. Or at least, they had offered security. Not enough. Whoever lived here had no chance of escaping a blade.

Small carved figurine toys remained sat atop the stone mantle; two larger faceless forms wrapped in pieces of hide around their torsos, then smaller figures with knitted rectangles tied onto them, forming draped dresses. Sigurd picked them up, stuffing them into the recesses of his leather trouser pockets. Children appealed to Sigurd, even if the claustrophobia of being settled didn't. He looked up to his much older sibling, with his fertile wife, and hoped that someday he too would enjoy the security of continuation of their family name. A part of him regretted near constant travelling. He had so far failed to secure a partner to bring sons to a hearth.

Sigurd moved into the next hovel and kept poking around. The guilty sense of intrusion grew alongside frustration.

"There's nothing," Arvan shouted down from the entrance stones. "Can't identify a church here either."

"And no great hall?" Rognval's deep voice started to sound resigned. He emerged from the dwelling he had been investigating with a face that spoke of his disappointment.

"Not that we can find, Lord," Arvan replied.

"Sigurd? Little brother, these people have nothing of value. Let's go," he commanded. They would have to get back in the boats and try again. Somewhere on this stretch of islands there must be what he sought. Glory in Valhalla would be so much sweeter if he knew he had provided well for his offspring before he went.

CHAPTER 2 – NATURAE

The belief-ribbons emanating from the crowds in the henge below wove around her body. Almost tangible to her eyes, Lana strained to feel the energy pulsing through her fingertips. As the chanting intensified, so too did the Lifeforce swirling through the ancient stone circle. She flapped and rose higher as if to tug the strands of Lifeforce up into herself. The tickling sensation as they followed her upwards made her smile with relief.

Sated finally, her enormous translucent wings lazily propelled her down again - although not so close that she could be seen from the stone circle. Hawk-like eyesight enabled her to pick out and identify the leaders of the humans below. She would log their attendance at the dawn ceremony later to remind her of whose lands to bless with life in the coming weeks. She frowned, realising that there seemed to be slightly fewer people here this morning. Perhaps a pestilence had struck one of the islands?

As rose-pink light filtered through the low clouds, the invisible haze of ribbons dissipated entirely. The spring sunlight began to cast long shadows through the sacred space. Dark hooded figures dampened the fires laid in the centre of the ancient ring of monoliths. Monotonous chanting in the henge petered out and the morning fell silent.

The resulting drop in energy signaled a cue - the Fae

Nobles, hovering above the stones, were now allowed to retreat. Disperse to their homelands and resume their shadowy existence. Lana, their Queen, did not bid them goodbye; their presence was necessary and tolerated, but she would never trust them entirely. Not since they had conspired to kill her mother nearly two-hundred years ago. She would have to endure their squabbles over lands and fickleness at Court in Naturae later anyway.

Lana looked down at the humans now plodding in file out of the henge. Flaming torches no longer required, they began to clap each other on shoulders, touch faces together and chatter amongst themselves. She could see from their fur-lined attire that her blessings to the lands continued to be bountiful. Well-rounded figures showed harvests and livestock flourished even in this harsh climate of the Northern Seas.

Lana dallied for a moment in the invisible apex of the stone circle. Despite her earlier satisfaction from the infusion of Lifeforce, watching the humans disperse in their little family groups made her feel hollow.

Lana's eyes followed a group of people who, having exited the ditches, were now hugging and conversing with a young couple on the tracks. The female proudly pushed forward a rounded belly and the man rubbed his hands over it. Lana suppressed a shudder of revulsion. In-vitro procreation - how peculiar these humans were. A small child barrelled into the family, yelling with his arms held up. Noisy, even after being picked up, he shouted about his displeasure and hunger.

But then, at least these mortals were not alone, as she was.

She was destined to be distant from her own offspring, such was the nature of how their ancient kind reproduced. With that pressing reminder of her daily need to bestow the newly gathered Lifeforce in the Pupaetory, Lana flew higher. Heading over the lochs, she allowed her wings to use the warm current to lift her above the clouds. Using the sun's position as guidance, she soared over the remaining lands to the sea, towards home. To Naturae, where everything was quiet and comfortingly controlled.

*****

Lana's adviser Lord Tolant was watching for her when she emerged from the Pupaetory, some hours later. His face was dark, unreadable, and his cheeks seemed paler than usual as he spoke.

"Your Highness," he stepped forward, choosing his words carefully so as not to alarm. "I - you - have been in receipt of a slightly disturbing report of late."

"Disturbing how?" Lana replied as the doors closed behind her. The cries of young fae ceased whining in her ears. She exhaled, purging herself of their burden. The pair of guards returned to patrolling the walkways encircling the building.

The Queen straightened her long sapphire blue gown whilst she waited for him to respond. She ran her eyes over Tolant's tatty attire. Bringing her slim hands up to her head, she checked her silver crown was still in place holding the cloud of black hair down. As he was clearly struggling to find the right words, she looked down her nose, saying, "I do wish you would find another robe to wear, Lord Tolant. That one has seen too many centuries of service."

"I have worn it proudly since before the Sation wars, your Highness."

"Well, see to it that one of the other workers fashion you a new one. As my most senior adviser, I expect you to at least look respectable."

"Your Highness," Tolant bowed again, "I have much to attend to, but I will, of course, find the time to make instructions for a fresh ceremonial gown."

"I'm sure I have asked you before," Lana said, "and yet you find time to advise me on a great many matters which I have no need of your input on. And still, when I ask you what your report contains, you have nothing to say?"

"Your Highness...Perhaps we should speak of this elsewhere?"

"Then why come and find me here? Just tell me Tolant and stop dithering. I am tired after blessing the vines and the flight after the ceremony. I must rest before court convenes."

"I know, my Queen, which is why I wanted to tell you before."

"Tell me what?" Really, the man was intolerable.

Tolant reluctantly handed her a tiny slip of curled manuscript, freshly released from a kestrel's leg. She drew in a breath as she saw the bloodstain on the corner. Before reading, she raised the small roll to her nose. Panic. Distress. Fear. Memories of missives from the Sation wars scattered across her mother's desk made her heart beat faster.

She read the hastily scribbled Faelore and her lips tightened.

Raiders - villagers dead or gone'

Lana narrowed her eyes at Tolant, who was studying the wooden planks. "Why am I only hearing of this now?"

Tolant continued inspecting the balcony floor. Suddenly enraged, she flew over to him and grasped his face, pulling it towards hers. "Why?"

His lips twisted, "Perhaps your spies should have...?" Her thin fingers shook his chin and she glared down at the weaselly adviser. Her keen eyes searched the darkness within his.

"There have been other reports, haven't there?"

Tolant flapped his wings and wrenched himself away from her grasp. Smoothing the front of his threadbare tunic, he drew himself up and jutted a pointy chin out. "I am but the bearer of this message, your Highness. That I intercepted it at all is purely happenstance." He made to bow and leave, but Lana landed next to him.

"Advise me now then," she said, forcing herself to swallow the ire. There were few enough fae which she trusted, and Tolant was at least competent, most of the time. His eyes slid away. Lana touched his arm, not seeing the slight twitch of his lips as he gazed out over the citadel close by.

Turning then with his face deliberately grave, he deferred,

"If your Highness would grant me permission to recall the spies, I am sure we will find out more. It is their job after all to blend in with the humans and observe."

Lana said reluctantly, "Very well."

Tolant bowed slightly and rounded to leave. She caught his arm, "I want to know why they failed to bring me information sooner. Is this the blood of a Noble? About their lands? Or just a general titbit? This scrap doesn't even say where this happened!"

Perhaps Tolant was right, her spies ought to have raised this to the Captain before it reached the point where a Noble had to send desperate messages by kestrel. She dropped his arm, pacing as she thought. Could this be the start of the Sation wars all over again? Surely not - vampires wouldn't have made the mistake of letting a kestrel away with evidence. Also, raiding wasn't their style, even if bloodshed was.

Tolant walked to the edge of the balcony. "I will try to find out what I can, your Highness." He unfurled his brown-tinted wings and flew away.

Lana clenched her fists, frustration and worry powering her wings as she soared up. Flying higher, she paused above the treetops, surveying Naturae beneath her. The palace was bathed in the warmth of early evening light. Spring leaves unrolled, a broken green camouflage for the structures nestling in the branches. Running from the central buildings, walkways bridged the trees and ladders ran to the ground. Pale outer constructs glowed as the last rays of sunshine hit the ancient wood, shouting almost of their unmaintained status.

Watching her dominion below, she hoped the sight would soothe her restless anxiety, but instead, the emptiness beneath reminded her of failure. Lana sighed and glanced back at the Pupaetory. Despite her long stint there today, she would return tomorrow. Endlessly giving of herself, her gathered Lifeforce, to bless the vines and make more workers. After the mass casualties of the Sation war, more soldiers, spies, workers for the palace and craft-fae were still needed. Naturae was replenishing but it took time. Worker lives were not eternal as hers and the Nobles were. And only a Queen can bless them, nurture them into existence, she mused. Just the one Queen. Never knowing if what she had created would be enough to endure whatever the future held. The lonely burden was overwhelming at times.

She looked over the mists to the setting sun on the seas, blending into horizon beyond. The day was not over yet, and as always, there was work to be done. Angry red streaks in the sky made her stomach clench like a stone, lurking and heavy. The stillness of the evening became uncomfortable, foreboding. She turned and flapped down, seeking company.

*****

Lana flew through the High Hall, above the assembled Nobles and Ambassadors below. Swooping through the lofty heights of the treetop chamber was her privilege alone. The crowd gathered on the mosaic Queendom map, which embellished the centre of the polished wood floor. Their feet obscured the detail deliberately out of respect - Lana's mother, the former Queen, had been murdered in front of her there. The blood stain over the north-west of England had never quite been completely removed. Although the Noble perpetrators had been banished, their kin remained - familial ties to their lands too political to entirely revoke. Lana could not bear to look at the map, too many painful memories. But neither could she cover it entirely, lest she forgot the lessons that day had taught her about trust.

When she alighted on the raised dais at the far end, they waited until she sat upon her throne, then swept down in homage. The room fell silent as she gazed over the finery bowing before her. Underneath capes wings rippled, waiting for her command to stand once more. She lifted a finger from the silver armrest and almost immediately a sigh of relief passed through the court. Chatter resumed. Lana counted their heads silently.

At least seven were not present, she estimated. Was this why there had been fewer humans at the ceremony? How did this relate to the note? The foreboding sensation from earlier returned, clenching at her insides. Her slim fingers beckoned behind her, and one of the two Queens Guard stepped closer, bending his helmeted head towards her. "Fetch the attendance roll," Lana whispered. "And bring it to my chambers." She stood, and announced, "Leave your offerings, I will acknowledge them later."

Leaving mouths agape - protocol was rarely altered - Lana swept out from the High Hall. Flying through empty wooden-paneled corridors until she reached the red doors at the end, she entered her rooms and sat, stifling her agitation, at her desk. The candles surrounding the edges of the surface were not yet lit. She sniffed in - out - quickly and tried not to allow the frustration rise. Slipping standards irked her. At least the workers had swept and dusted today.

A quiet knock at the door. "Enter," she commanded. The Queen's Guard stood in the ornate aperture, his green uniform contrasting to the rich red of the wooden doorway. At her slight nod, he silently proffered the scroll and bowed.

With no acknowledgement of his service, Lana untied the lace binding the attendance log together. She moved to the wide window to catch the last of the light as she examined the neatly noted names. Satisfied that her earlier estimation was correct, she rummaged through smaller scrolls in a basket underneath the desk until she found the map. The messy pile bothered her and she couldn't help but order them back precisely in place. Then she felt calm enough to unroll the picture on her desk.

Less intricately designed than the large marquetry map on the High Hall floor, this vellum marked Noble family names adjacent to their designated lands. Her mother had scrawled through those who died in the Sation wars, and only one third of the ancient families now remained. The Nobles absent from Court today governed the isles of Sanday and Eday. Lord Essenthal was from close to this island of Naturae - the village of Pierowall. Too close.

She looked up - the guard was still there, awaiting dismissal. "Fetch the Captain," she ordered. He disappeared off into the hallways, nearly colliding with a worker in his haste. The woman squeaked and fluttered in, hesitating as she realised the Queen was in her rooms, rather than Court. Her drab tunic splattered with wax from the slender candle she was cradling, she had the sense to look down, ready for her admonishment. Lana narrowed her eyes but with a slight nod, granted her permission to belatedly light the chamber. Lana prepared herself for a long night of worrying and administration.

CHAPTER 3 - THE REQUEST

Sigurd thrust his blade deep into the feisty youth before him, then kicked him off to retract. The lad fell backwards, splayed on the beach. A single bubble of blood escaped his mouth as he breathed his last. Wiping the remains of entrails from the sharp edge as he turned, Sigurd caught sight of the tussle behind him.

Arvan was laughing as Rognval was engaged with a farmer of similar height to him wielding, of all things, a wooden pitchfork. Sigurd almost smirked himself except that he could see the farmer - or someone else maybe - had already somehow struck a blow to his brother. Red oozed down his left leg with every movement, staining the fur on his boots. Rognval was favouring his right so clearly the wound was deep enough to cause him bother.

Sigurd hovered close by. Only honour and the stern talking to Rognval had given him earlier stopped him from intervening. This was surely an unfair match, he decided. Breath-Slayer should be able to snap the pitchfork easily, if only the peasant wasn't nimbly dodging away. The muscled islander persisted with his strategy of duck and poke, weaving away from a tiring Yarl.

Sigurd dithered, restlessly shuffling his weight between his feet, his hand automatically fondling the silver Thor's

Hammer he wore around his neck. Perhaps Rognval had been right; he was usually too quick to dive in where it wasn't necessary. Today, now, he tried instead to rein in his impulses, rather than lunge in to put a swift end to the islander's pointless yet valiant fight.

Just then, with a roar, Rognval ran straight at the man. He stopped just before his bewildered opponent, pivoted low on his right foot and, using his long sword, sliced the farmer at his calves. The pitchfork's end caught on the ground and the tall man's knees caved. Rognval completed the turn, somewhat lumbering for balance but bringing Breath-Slayer down on exposed neck. A brief gurgle and the farmer lay still.

Breathing heavily, Rognval looked up at his audience. Politely standing in a circle, his crew and family raised their swords in acknowledgement of his victory. Rognval sank to the sand on his knees, his face twisted with pain. This was no moment of celebration. He clenched his teeth, knowing something sinister was sweeping through his body with every heartbeat.

"I'll sort out the rest, don't worry brother." Sigurd clapped his hand on Rognval's shoulder.

"Go find a Church," Rognval panted out. "Make sure you get there first."

"We cannot fit more slaves, I know," Sigurd said reassuringly. Arvan had already begun ferreting through the dead for jewellery. With any luck, they would be heading home within a few hours. Sigurd loped off, then glanced back at Rognval, expecting a grin of acknowledgement that he was making the right choices today.

"Go!" Rognval commanded, pointing his finger. "The day is young yet!" The grin was more of a grimace.

*****

Sigurd returned to the shoreline to find Rognval where he left him, except now laid flat on his back. He looked flushed and his breathing laboured. Dropping the trinkets he had bundled in a rag, Sigurd rushed to his side. Dismayed, he felt his brother's torso, pulling at the fastenings and tearing open his fur and leather tabard. Rognval grunted and raised his arm slightly away from his left side. Blood started to seep out as soon as the restrictive laces fell away. He moaned, beckoning Sigurd to come closer.

"Stay," Rognval panted. "Take the lands here."

Sigurd swallowed but couldn't stop the tears welling up. He shook his head, "No, we need to get you home."

Rognval closed his eyes and turned his head away.

"Please brother, Erika will know what to do. What medicine to give you, to make this right?"

Rognval opened his eyes and stared at Sigurd. The pale blue so familiar to Sigurd seemed to glow as he whispered, "Pass me Breath-Slayer."

Sigurd reached over his kin and, grasping Rognval's hand, placed it firmly on the wound on the torso. "Press," he instructed with a confidence he did not feel. "I will get bindings and we will get home."

Rognval smiled. "Breath-Slayer." The order was firm.

"No!" Sigurd pleaded, "I will be quick!"

He shouted over his shoulder, "Prepare the boats! We leave for home now!"

Casting his eyes around the beach, Sigurd realised that he was alone with Rognval. The others were still searching the homesteads. He could hear their laughter on the winds gently drifting over from the shallow dunes beyond.

"Arvan! Torv!" He bellowed again. He held his own hand over Rognval's, but the warm blood was still seeping out through his fingertips at an alarming rate. His brother's life soaking slowly into the sand. Sigurd felt around behind him for his brother's sword. Frustrated, he turned about and shuddered as he took in the enormous patch of red pooling around Rognval's calf.

A chill washed over him, and he couldn't catch his breath. Not knowing what else to do, he kept blinking away the shock of what was about to happen. His hands searched the sand as if someone else were moving them. All of a sudden, Sigurd felt as if he was receding into himself, becoming very small and insignificant.

His fingers finally touched the cold metal, nicking him as he picked up the blade. He slapped it down onto Rognval's chest. Part of him considered refusing this one comfort, as if by denying it, Rognval would somehow battle on. But he couldn't do that to him, couldn't defy his order. Could not bring himself to invoke the wrath of the gods by withholding something so precious to his brother.

Rognval smiled and removed his hand from his ribs, grasping at the hilt. His breathing grew more ragged. Sigurd stared at the vivid red which now seemed to spurt out of the hole. Rognval grasped Sigurd's wrist with his other hand - the contact jolted Sigurd back into the present, but it was a hopeless, powerless one.

Sigurd cast his eyes frantically around the beach, shouting again and again, but only the slaves, still chained on the boats, responded. Their heads poked over the low sides watching. Faces pulled into gnarled smiles as they watched their captors suffer.

Sigurd said, "Why aren't they coming?" He blinked, as much from the sand and drizzle as tears.The beach had fallen quiet, not even seagulls screamed. Only the distant rattle of the waves pulling shale could be heard.

"Promise me, you will stay. Settle here little brother. Good land."

The gruff, slowly spoken words tore at Sigurd. Bowing his head, the tears ran freely, dropping onto Rognval's armour. He shook his head. Dreadlocks fell over his shoulders and knocked at Rognval's chest, dipping in the slowing pool of blood running from his wound.Sigurd bit his lip, perhaps the pain there would ease the rising ache in his ribcage.

"Promise me. You will be Yarl..." Rognval's broken voice had an urgency now which Sigurd understood.

"I don't want to be Yarl...you are Yarl, you are my rock."

Sigurd gazed into his brother's eyes, desperate for him to understand that he couldn't leave, he must fight on.

But Rognval gripped his wrist harder, digging his nails in as if assuming that pain would be more compelling than the heartache he was now causing his little brother. "Promise me..." Rognval croaked, the bubble from his lips barely forming before it burst. "Stay and settle, for once in your life...just do what I say."

Sigurd felt as if he was hearing someone else, watching them, as they declared the words, "I will." Then, with a jolt, the comfort this last wish from his brother would provide dawned on him. "We will," he said with more conviction.

With a sigh and a slight smile, Rognval clutched his sword hilt and prepared for Valhalla.

CHAPTER 4 – SPY

Lana flounced into the empty High Hall, kicking a chair out of the way as she stomped towards the dais. The midsummer ceremony she had just returned from had been dissatisfying. She was still hungry, and Tolant's simpering platitudes as they had flown back were beginning to annoy her.

"Fetch me the spies for Rousay," she ordered, knowing he would have followed her in.

Dithering, Tolant protested, "That will take time, your Highness."

"I know!" Lana screeched. "I am waiting, so get a move on!"

Tolant scurried from the hall. Lana collapsed into her throne and tried to gather herself. Her Queens Guard entered from behind her, and she could sense their twitchiness. Her jaws tightened - they were right to fear her. In this mood, she didn't even know herself how she would react.

"Order sustenance," she said, calming herself by arranging her skirt neatly. One of them quietly disappeared. Tolant strode back in through the double doors, a worried look upon his face.

"Well?"

"I have issued the order to return to submit their reports, your Highness, but..."

"But what? Did you not think this situation would require immediate action?"

Tolant stopped in his tracks and studied the floor.

"You should have left the ceremony as soon as it was apparent barely any humans were there!"

"Your Highness, I felt it was more important to support you..." Tolant mumbled but resumed his approach.

"This is the second time the henges have been half empty. I need to know - where are the people?"

"I understand your frustration, your Highness, I am doing my best to find the answers!"

Lana thumped the arm of her throne, then stood. Wheeling around, she ordered the remaining guard to fetch the Captain.

A worker fae entered, wrestling with a young deer in his arms. Lana pursed her lips in anticipation. Usually she didn't need to bother with live animals, but her appetite hadn't been quelled by Lifeforce from this latest ceremony. She grabbed the beast by the scuff of its neck and inhaled. Youthful energy spurred on by panic drove the deer to wriggle and buck. The worker had the good sense to grasp its kicking rear legs as the Queen bent over and pierced the strong muscles.

Greedily, she sucked the blood and Lifeforce, not caring about how she must look. Tolant watched on indulgently, hoping her mood would improve with sustenance. He had lately taken to keeping a supply of live yet malleable animals close at hand. His knowledge of the forests of Naturae, the flora and fauna, had built up over decades of managing them.

Lana drank deeply, savouring the rich tones of the forest life the creature had enjoyed. Immediately, her skin began to luminesce and her eyes brightened. It wasn't the same sensation as worship provided, but it was close enough to quell some of her hunger.

With the animal drained until only a furry bag of bones remained, Lana raised her head. She licked her mouth. The worker passed over a small cloth and she delicately wiped her face. Bowing then bundling the carcass under one arm, the fae still looked nervous as he retreated. Lana's eyes glittered - although partially sated, the heady rush from her infusion meant she wasn't fully in control of herself just yet. All fae knew the moments just after death happened were dangerous. The urge to hunt pulled strongly. Most fae learned early in life how to suppress the feeling, to pace themselves, but the Queen was unreliable in that regard.

Tolant turned away from assessing his Queen as footsteps approached. "Captain," he greeted, "I believe the Queen would be ready to hear your report now."

Lana sat upright in the throne, her eyes skimmed over the light flying armour adorning the fae before her. The Captain nodded, his stubby brown wings fluttering behind him, betraying his nerves. The Captain's voice was firm and clear however.

"As ordered, we have increased the patrols around Naturae and, as such, have no unusual activity to report. The status of the mist remains high and I am confident we are still cloaked."

Lana studied the middle-aged fae commander. He had served her diligently for decades - from pupaetory to the drill room, his life had been preordained. Groomed to soldier.

Now he led her army and oversaw the spy network, and he had always appeared competent. But the days of peace were possibly fast fading, and he was untested in battle.

"The guard-fae, they have doubled their training time as well as patrolling?" Lana leaned forward.

"As directed, your Highness."

Tolant shot a glance at the Queen, "I think we can rely on our Captain to tell us immediately of any encounters they have on our shores."

Lana's eyes narrowed. "I hope your confidence in the shielding from the mists is justified. Who knows what powers these invaders possess?"

There was a quiet cough from the far end of the High Hall. In the aperture, a short, slight young fae with messy-looking black hair looked at the group near the dais and waited. He wore human attire, although his slender brown wings were visible. With his youthful face, Issam would appear to humans aged in his second decade, when he was actually nearer to his fifth. Tolant beckoned him to approach.

"Your Highness, this is the spy, known as Issam," Tolant said.

"Which lands do you cover?" Lana asked. All fae spies came from the same vine, which resulted in facial similarities and encouraged loyalty to each other as well as the Queendom. Like all fae, their role was determined before they even left the cocoon.

Issam's eyes darted to the Captain, who silently approved this breaking cover. A royal audience demanded bending of certain rules.

"Broch, usually," Issam answered respectfully. "On Rousay."

"Report," the Captain ordered.

Issam looked through brown eyelashes at the Queen. He hardly dared to believe he was here, in her presence. In a low voice, he spoke clearly, as if he had been rehearsing on his journey.

"Invaders have settled on the lands. They number perhaps sixty on Rousay. The men are giants, swift of foot and sword. Many have markings on their bodies and faces. They also are proficient with arrows and spear. The farmers and craftsmen have mostly been kept as their prisoners, but they have put some back to work on the lands. Closely guarded at all times though. Other than that labour, the islanders have no freedom. They sleep in tent structures which the foreign people constructed inside the animal enclosures."

"Who are these 'men' you speak of?" Lana asked.

"They came in long boats with tall carved curls on each end," Issam replied. "The boats landed directly on the beaches and quickly overran the homesteads. I didn't witness it myself - I only overheard conversations amongst those who they took captive. Many humans died. Taken by surprise, they couldn't arm themselves in time to resist."

"And what of the Nobles? Why have they not returned to seek assistance, or let us know what happened?"

Issam looked at the floor. He shrugged, "The men from the boats have fearsome weapons. They kill without hesitation. I saw them burn the bodies of the humans, maybe they caught the Nobles also?" Issam began to mumble now, unsure.

"When did you last see the Nobles?" Lana asked.

Issam studied the floor intently.

"Answer your Queen!" Tolant prompted.

"I have not seen any Nobles since before the men in the boats arrived." Issam finally said. "But I don't usually anyway. They keep themselves very much hidden."

Lana said, "They are supposed to be our link with the humans, honoured elders who can advise. Encourage the humans to the ceremonies, to worship. Have they not been doing that?"

Tolant's eyes shifted away, before changing the subject. "Where did the boats come from? Does anyone know?"

"They speak in a strange tongue, Lord. I have not heard it before. They have rituals as well, paint themselves and chant." Issam volunteered.

"That does not explain where they are from and why they have come," Tolant said.

The Captain interrupted, "He is young, your Highness, this is his first posting. We cannot expect him to know about the origins of these strangers. They could have come from anywhere."

Turning back to Issam, Lana asked, "What rituals? What magic do they possess? Are they part of the new religion? The one with the cross?" Her wings began to flap in agitation and she paced away. The three workers looked at each other and shrugged behind her back. Better not to say anything if you didn't definitively know.

Lana turned back, and frowned. "Not only have the

Nobles who could tell us this conveniently disappeared, instead of protecting their lands as they ought. But," she said, picking at her nails, as she turned to face them, "they have allowed invaders to retain our humans." She sighed, "It doesn't sound like these new humans are vampires at least. Do they have any organisation? A leader perhaps?"

Issam shook his head, "I cannot tell for sure, your Highness."

She stood up, wandered down the steps. "I cannot help but think we need to know more." Lana looked at Tolant, raising an eyebrow.

Tolant nodded, "Yes, send out a search party to find the Nobles. Captain?"

"No," Lana interrupted. "More about the invaders." She glared at Tolant. Swallowing down her fear of treason and change, Lana straightened and held her head high. Turning to Issam and the Captain, she ordered, "You will send a small raiding force to capture one of these giant men. Preferably one who seems important to them. A leader, an elder, someone they respect. Bring him here, maybe we can learn more."

The Captain gulped but nodded curtly. The order was skirting the fringes of what was permissible, possible even, but he dared not question it.

Issam said quietly, "There is a man, he spends time alone. I've seen him telling the other men what to do. He walks on the beaches, especially after they burned one of their own there."

The Queen smiled, "You have done well Issam, make sure

you take sustenance while the Captain assembles his team. You shall lead them back and identify this individual to them, then remain there and observe. I expect regular reports from you."

She flew up and towards the double doors, leaving them shooting glances at each other with wary eyes. She called back, "It is completely unacceptable that our ways be ignored. The humans must return to the ceremonies. If those Nobles cannot manage, then I will find others who can!"

Issam opened his mouth to speak in defence of the imprisoned humans, but after a warning glance from the Captain, closed it again. Tolant smirked and followed the Queen out.

CHAPTER 5 - CAPTIVE

Sigurd stood on a low dune facing the sea. The weight of the little silver hammer pulling on his neck seemed greater as he contemplated his situation. He massaged its edges, acknowledging the weight had been more pressing since Rognval had gone. There were few objects or people which he cared about, but this hammer was more than a token, it was the badge of belonging, however reluctantly.

In his pockets, he still carried the wooden toys from the first village they had raided in these distant shores. Something about their innocence appealed to him at the time, the simplicity of childhood play perhaps. But now, they had become a reminder that Rognval wanted him to settle here, perhaps raise a family of his own. He considered throwing them into the sea, not yet ready to make that commitment, but not willing to reject his promise either. The thoughts and desires jumbled in his mind, sometimes overwhelmingly, and confusion over the right way forward frequently caused him to act in ways which others thought peculiar. They made sense to him at the time though.

Conflicted, Sigurd repeatedly scanned the horizon, half expecting the answer to appear from what lay beyond. Wind whipped his dreadlocks around his head as he inhaled. He closed his eyes and splayed his arms, feeling the freedom of a breeze on his face and hands. The salty tang of the ocean moistened his lips, and he smiled.

Then, the wind began to buffet him from all sides. As quickly as his mind processed the change, and ordered his eyes to open, he was enveloped by darkness. Confused, he tried to bring his hands up to remove whatever was obscuring his sight. Cool metal encircled his wrists. Then his arms were tugged behind him. The metal fastened tighter.

"Get off!" His words sounded thick through the covering. "Get off me!"

Hands grabbed him under the arms - through his furs he could feel the pressure of fingers gripping tightly. He tried to wriggle away, banking on his strength to enforce his captors to lose their grip. But, horrifyingly, as he moved his legs to kick, he felt the unnerving sensation of carrying his own weight. His foot returned to where the ground should be, but met nothing. He kicked out again but his leg felt weightless, untethered. Then his ankles were caught and he was pulled, splayed face down.

Cool air rippled over the skin on his stomach as his clothes untucked. He shook his head to try to remove whatever it was draped over. His movements caused the tugs on his arms to strengthen their grip, pulling him to ever straighter limbs. The weight of his torso wrenched painfully on his hips and shoulders.

Sigurd paused in his attempts to free himself as realisation dawned. An odd sensation of weightlessness in the pit of his stomach and the beating wind he felt on his back, akin to the lurching sensation of a boat falling down the crest of a wave.

Sigurd resisted the urge to throw up. He was airborne. Something was carrying him through the air.

Inside the head cover, he stuck his tongue out. He could feel the fabric pushed against his face as the propulsion moved against it. He ran his tongue over the course material, his spit immediately felt cold by the time he next ran his tongue over it. The taste of salt was strong. Was he flying over the sea or was it remnants of the beach?

He tried to hear past the rush of air as the rhythmic beating carried on. The beats were so fast, faster than a birds. Were they wings? Even the Gods - mysterious yet humanoid - had no need of wings. Frigga - wife of Odin himself, Queen of the Æsir, and goddess of the sky, didn't use wings. What kind of magic was holding him then? He tried not to panic - place his faith in the gods for their mercy.

He listened for the sounds of waves, or people, or grass - anything to get a bearing on where he was. He hoped it was the sea. Water promised a less certain death than being dropped from a height to the ground.

He heard nothing - not even a comforting slap of waves. Then he inwardly kicked himself - the sea is largely silent of course, unless it hits an obstacle.

No way of knowing. Wherever he was, he wanted to conserve his energy for when this nauseating weightlessness stopped. There was no point in fighting an enemy you couldn't see or touch. You cannot win without a scrap of information to tell you where you, or they, were. He closed his eyes and tried to imagine what Valhalla would look like when he made it there.

*****

A sudden, damp chill permeated through to his skin, then Sigurd could feel they were slowing down through the air. His body was pulled off kilter, having been horizontal the whole time. It was almost as disorientating as getting airborne had been. Then, a jerk to his shoulders told him his bearers landed and immediately started walking. He tensed his back and stomach muscles as the pulling on his arms slackened and his torso started to sag. His back straightened and he clenched his stomach muscles. Tried to draw in his limbs but the grip on them remained firm. Gritting his teeth, he drew his muscles even more taut. He felt a slight give on his left wrist before a blow landed on his elbow, forcing a release as the pain shot up his arm.

They were still moving at a steady pace. The skin on his stomach grew slightly warmer now that air was no longer buffeting against its bareness. His ears picked out the rustle of trees and the slight chink of metal on metal as his assailants progressed. Also, quiet panting.

Birds didn't pant. Animals did. Winged metallic animals with hands? Sigurd was utterly confused. Nothing in his years of exploration had ever exposed him to something akin to this.

The moving motion paused. A command barked in a strange tongue. The response sounded almost lyrical, like the ones the villagers used but had a different inflection. He had only been on those islands for less than a moon cycle, and hadn't yet bothered to pick up much beyond a few phrases, preferring to avoid talking to the people here. Blaming them unilaterally for his brother's death.

He cursed Rognval for bringing them on this foolish raid. Immediately he wished he hadn't. But he was tied into a deathbed promise to settle on the windy shores. Were the gods displeased that his heart wasn't in it? Was this their retribution?

A shock wave of pain drove through his legs as he was dropped to the ground. Head covering ripped off but his eyes couldn't recover quickly enough in the darkness to see much immediately. Although his wrists were still being held, his legs kicked out, hoping to trip one of them up. Dirt underfoot - he felt the drag as his boot pulled through the soil but no sound.

He blinked, the darkness made it difficult to focus. Wrestling again, pulling against the constraints around his wrists. The fingers gripping his arms disappeared. His eyes adjusted to the dimness, making out out shadowy figures. They were moving, stretching the ropes around his wrists tighter as they retreated.

His arms were pulled higher, stretched apart. The ropes chafed next to his hands and he was forced to stand. Lumbering to his feet to relieve the tension which was now yanking his wrists.

"Argh!" Sigurd yelped. When he closed his mouth after the scream, something was blocking it. His mouth was then forced back open, held open with the coldness that could only be metal. Gloved hands felt inside his mouth, around his teeth gently. Vulnerable and exposed, Sigurd stopped squirming. They lifted his lips, pulling them to expose his gums. Then, as quickly as it had been placed, the obstruction was removed. He spat to clear the dirty leathery taste from his tongue.

They dropped the covering back on his head. "No," he pleaded, "Take it off!" He started to shake his head, as if jerking it would somehow remove the offensive restriction. "Take it off, show yourselves!"

Silence. Only the faintest whisper of wind told him they were leaving. A deep thud of a door. Then a scrape and a click.

But they hadn't all left. He could sense at least one other person still there with him. Watching him.

CHAPTER 6 - TORTURE

Lord Tolant's chambers were small but well ordered. He, like his Queen, preferred everything placed in a certain location. His possessions, few that they were, were proudly displayed. Each held significance for him, a visual reminder of how far he had progressed through the fae hierarchy. Traditions and history were to be valued. Without them, anarchy threatened. And anarchy was no respecter of position.

Reaching along the shelves which lined the far wall of his rooms for his set of implements, he remembered the power he had felt when last wielding them. As the former Lord of the Beneath, with the title of Lord Anaxis even though he was not a Noble, he had been responsible for many a prisoner's confessions during the war. So skilled was he with the blades, that he could extract the darkest of secrets, from all manner of creatures. Negligent fae, stupid vampires, and even the weaker halflings - humans who somehow had imbibed their lines with magic but had no clue as to what they were, or of the powers they wielded. The humans called them witches or daemons. To him, they were just anomalies.

Placing the leather wrap on the bed, he unrolled it. These beautiful tools had been largely dormant since his rise. Almost reverently, Tolant pulled out his personal instruments. A slim, silver-plated blade, curved to finish in the narrowest of tips. A beautiful weapon with so many uses. An exquisite tiny clamp - fashioned from hardwood points which flexed slightly when a finger was pulled, whilst the metal strip embedded in the curve provided the force to keep it firmly in place. Tolant stroked the smooth ring, enjoying the texture as much as the intended purpose of the equipment.

Yes, a part of him missed the Sation Wars greatly. However, he much preferred, now he was of advancing age, the stability which the return to order had provided. He supported the Queen as best he could, and she had repaid him with increasing trust and responsibility. Lowly Tolant, a worker from a respected soldier vine, had survived. Promoted out of the Beneath when the old Queen died. Promoted with pride, he admitted to himself. Rewarded for his hard work.

He looked up at the trinkets on his shelves again, remembering each gift from her and valuing its significance. The goblet - crafted for the occasion of her first century reigning Naturae. The early years of her reign had not been smooth, but for two centuries now he had stood by her side. Even though Tolant had not known of what would happen to her mother, the opportunity the coup presented for him personally was unparalleled. But, then again...the old Queen had become the lone, dissenting voice when the other Fae Queendoms were surrendering to the vampires. Her demise was, to his mind, inevitable. She hadn't followed the rules. Lana must not be allowed to make the same mistake.

He stroked the deep yellow sash which he wore to the Council meetings, probably his most prized possession. No other worker fae had ever sat on the Council, and he felt that his delicate balancing of the Queen's needs and keeping the Nobles happy was the only way to maintain order. Quite rightly, Queen Lana mistrusted the Council at first, but with his encouragement, they maintained the traditional systems. These structures, mostly for communication, had worked for thousands of years prior to the decades of the Sation Wars. Tolant passionately believed they would work for thousands more.

Indeed, he had always said it was unfortunate it was that a princess should ascend so early in her life. But, very fortunate for him, Tolant acknowledged as he rolled up the wrap.

Now, his mind turned to this new threat. He supposed he should try to find out exactly what manner of creature or human he was. Lana knew that the other information he provided was of the most reliable quality. He did not intend to let his Queen down now. This minor matter should not interrupt what had otherwise been a peaceful reign. She could depend on him to ensure the security of Naturae, no matter what.

*****

Chilly tunnels led down to the cells underneath the citadel. Deep within the roots of the ancient trees which supported the buildings, neither the light nor the warmth of the sun penetrated. One had to navigate from memory, unless a guard had been remiss and left the small fish oil candles burning in tiny hollows down the passageway walls. Fae did not need light to see in the darkness, their night vision was incomparable. The lamps were purely used for comfort, a token nod to civilisation. There was only one way in and out - although routes from the entrance also diverted to the worker camps.

Tolant knew the twisting paths well of course, despite having had no need to venture into them for decades. He had grown used to living above - not just above those unfortunates who resided in the encampments on the outskirts of the island, but in the vastly superior accommodations of the Palace. Still, he grew comfortable quickly with the familiar earthy environment. Little changes, he thought, sniffing the peat and decay.

Outside one of the cells, he was met by the young Captain. A fae he had lent his support to as he advanced through the ranks of the soldiers, Tolant trusted that he would have chosen only the best of his warriors to guard the prisoner.

"Well done on a successful capture," Tolant smiled. The Captain nodded, "The spy's information was correct. We were able to snatch him with little problem."

"And what is your assessment?" It never hurt to get another viewpoint.

"He is very strong," the Captain conceded. "I have heard him compared to a vampire in that regard, amongst the men. Not that many of them have ever captured a vampire of course."

"Indeed," Tolant said, his mouth pursed. "Did you check his teeth?"

"The first thing we did, my Lord."

"Human?"

"As far as we could ascertain."

"Good. It would be very, very problematic if we had taken a vampire." Tolant shook his head. Very dangerous indeed should it become known they had a vampire on Naturae.

"Can I rely on your guards to keep him steady whilst I ask my questions?"

The Captain's eyes slid over to Tolant's. He knew of his reputation. This would be the first time he would see it in action however. The young commander nodded, his face completely devoid of emotion.

Good, thought Tolant, it didn't look like the Captain was going to start spouting any nonsense about the sanctity of human life either. Tolant didn't intend for it to get that far; information was what he wanted. What happened after that would be up to the Queen to take responsibility for.

"Unlock the cell then please."

The Captain pulled out a large black key and fitted it into the crude but effective lock. In the darkness of the cell, two fae soldiers stood guard. Tolant brought in a lamp so that the prisoner could see his instruments.

Tolant studied the figure in the gloom. He looked almost peaceful, his head slumped back against the earth walls of the cell. He would be tall when standing - at the moment his legs were splayed out across the floor. He was pinned to the wall by his arms which were pulled out and held by ropes. His clothing looked warm - furs tied around his chest with thin thongs, and encasing his feet also. There looked to be a woven undergarment, the flaps of which could be seen around his midriff. On his arm, a few silver circlets rounded the impressive width of his bicep. Strong indeed.

Tolant set his wrap down, untied it and drew out the curved blade. He flicked his eyes back to the prisoner, and knew that the man was pretending not to notice their presence. A tiny twitch of his whiskers betrayed him. Tolant smiled to himself.

"Pull him up," he commanded the guards. A whisper of the thin metal rope straining as it tightened through the hoops in the walls. The man struggled to maintain his pretence at sleeping but did not make a sound. The stretch alone of his arms must have hurt, Tolant knew.

The man's eyes flew open and he looked straight at Tolant. Bright blue eyes bored into him and the man snarled. Tolant's mouth began to sneer as they sized each other up.

A halfling. Not his first encounter with one, Tolant had met them on the battlefield before. But this one - this one was different. He could smell the strangeness of him, like the smell after lightening struck. This one was oddly...compelling.

Tolant felt deep in his body that the man was dangerous. Not the kind of danger which a vampire might pose with their strength and speed. But the sort which was beguiling. Chaotic. Interesting and exciting. Possessed of an innate attractiveness to fae-kind. One which would send fae crazed for more. Overrule the restraint which was learnt after hunting.

Then he realised that the beautiful blade he held would be unsuitable. This man's blood should not be spilt. The magic within it would only command the wrong kind of response.

The Captain might trust his guards, but if there was daemon blood around then no fae could be trusted. However, he showed the man the polished knife regardless, his thin lips twisted into a smile as the halfling's eyes bulged.

"Tighten his ropes."

Tolant broke off the stare and reached over for his finger clamp. He rolled it around in the palm of his hands. The shape comforted him, reassuring him that there were other ways to get the information he wanted.

Using the blade, as the man's torso was pulled up, Tolant slid the knife under the bindings holding the jacket together. So smooth was the cut, the man looked down in surprise at the sudden release of his chest. Tolant was close enough to get drenched by the man's spittle as he roared.

Undeterred by the noise, Tolant then slashed the thongs holding the leggings around his waist. He was careful to pull the blade away from the skin before pulling - relying on the sharpness to slice when the pressure was too much for the leather to resist. The leg coverings were so thick and stiff from sweat they did not fall as expected. The tip of the knife hooked just below the halflings belly hole dropped them down past his knees. Slowly, so the man would know the blade was near his precious groin area. The blade must not nick his skin, just the promise of that possibility was enough.

Tolant watched his hand moving with such precision and care, it was almost like he was watching someone else. Age had not diminished his exquisite control. As the trousers dropped, two small carved objects with bits of leather tied around their middles, fell out of a pocket.

The man snarled and said something in a language Tolant did not know. Tolant looked up, slightly surprised. Not at the words, but at the note of pain which the release of these objects seemed to cause. The tone of the word implied they had importance to him.

Picking them up, Tolant examined them. He had heard of items having power, perhaps even being the source of the power, for some halflings. Was it that easy? He held up the wooden pieces to the man's face and watched for a reaction.

The man stoically recovered his glare, but, he chewed on his lip a little. He blinked and looked once at the objects, then stared at Tolant again. An edge of insolence had crept into his expression. Tolant's thin lips curled in victory.

What else would he find out, he wondered? His appetite for torture had barely even been whetted. Tolant licked his lips and showed the man the finger clamp. The man absorbed the small circle and then, rather surprisingly, laughed. He spat again, then looked at Tolant as he let out an unintelligible torrent of words. All of which sounded like defiance to Tolant.

Tolant waited until the man expended the last of his energy on what no doubt was vague threats to himself, and probably rude remarks about his lineage, stature, whatever else offended the man about himself or his situation. Since it was clear that any form of discussion would be irrelevant given their language barrier, he decided to simply indulge himself. A skills refresher, he justified. The man had already yielded as much information as he realistically could from his reactions to the power objects being removed. Tolant didn't think this simple creature, violent and strong, but still only a halfling, would be capable of impacting the Queendom's security.

Decision made, he turned to the onlookers, saying with no small amount of relish in his voice, "I will also need the knotted leather swatches, Captain, if you don't mind sending for them. And perhaps, yes, perhaps a training staff as well."

Tolant pushed up his sleeves and began.

CHAPTER 7– THE INTERVIEW

Lana paced up and down her chambers. "Enter," she said as soon as she heard the knock. The doors opened slowly and Tolant slid in. He closed the door behind him, taking his time to ensure they were properly shut before he swivelled around to meet her anxious stare.

"Well?"

Tolant placed his hands together and advanced into the room with his head inclined. He stood by the window and gazed out, seemingly absorbed in the stars.

"Tell me!" Lana almost screeched. "Do we have one?"

Tolant turned and his face darkened. "We do, your Highness."

"And? What has he said? Have you 'questioned' him?"

A small lifting of his thin lips. "In as much as one can question someone who does not speak our language, yes."

Lana clenched her fists. Really, the man was intolerable. She took a breath and calmly said, "So what information *do* we have?"

Tolant replied, "The man is a simple barbarian. I see no further purpose in trying to elicit anything from him."

"Does he have magic? Or is he just an ordinary human?"

Tolant smirked at this, "Oh, I believe your Highness would find him quite without magic. He appears too dim-witted enough to wield it. His behaviour is... erratic."

"I want to see him for myself."

Tolant's eyes widened, "Oh no, your Highness, I do not think that is wise."

"What have you tried? To get him to tell us what he wants?"

Turning back to the window, Tolant said, "Oh, I tried all the usual implements." For a moment there was silence as he appeared lost in the memory of it. Then, he faced her, eyes narrowed. "He was not co-operative. Even when we asked him with brute force."

Lana looked down at her hands. "And is he still alive?"

"Barely."

"Then I will see him. Have him brought to the High Hall. I will not descend to the Beneath. Perhaps I can make headway on finding out his intentions."

"It is not wise to entertain prisoners, I urge you to reconsider your Highness. Your safety..."

Lana waved her hand in dismissal. "I hardly think he will be able to harm me. I have seen the state you left prisoners in when you were Lord of the Beneath."

"Your Highness, there is no need for your involvement."

Lana's eyes flashed. "On this, we disagree. I cannot have the stability of this realm upset." She walked towards her desk and picked up the map. "So far we have 'lost' seven Nobles from court. Whether they are still alive remains to be determined."

She shook the map at Tolant. "The humans are not attending the ceremonies! I cannot perform my duties without

Lifeforce. At what point do you think.." She drew in a deep breath, aware that she was on the verge of pent up fury boiling over. "That I *should* get involved?"

Throwing the map to the floor, she glared at her adviser. Tolant met her eyes evenly before bending down to retrieve the manuscript.

He blinked slowly. "I maintain, your Highness, that the barbarian poses a threat. To you personally. To your Queendom. He needs to be finished. He can never leave Naturae, he knows of us now." Tolant's eyes slid away, knowing what he was proposing her endorsement of went against everything that had been agreed since the end of the Sation wars.

"I am not for one moment suggesting he leaves! You know he must not be allowed to die. Not until I know what their intentions are!" Lana stamped her foot. How dare this upstart challenge her so?

"Bring him to me! I will handle this now. You have done enough." Lana's enormous wings unfurled from behind her and she began to hover. Tolant dipped his head before turning and retreating.

Lana turned to look out of the window. In truth, she was a little excited to meet a barbarian. She wondered whether there would be something of help in the Scriptaerie. Perhaps the reports from the Sation wars held some clues as to overcoming a language barrier? All of the Ambassadors which used to attend court during her mother's time spoke their language, but she knew they had travelled from far away to reach Naturae. They would be her last resort to ask though.

Her mind made up, she flew out to the corridor and down to the Scriptaerie.

CHAPTER 8 – FROM ON HIGH

The High Hall was empty bar her Queens Guard. Emboldened with an idea gleaned from a report in the Scriptaerie, Lana flew up to lurk in the high white arches of the eaves. She remained, looking down the chamber towards the throne.

As ordered by the Captain, the soldiers silently formed a line along the dais. A gleaming wall of silver and green would be the barbarian's first impression. Identical in every way. Lana smiled to herself and raised her chin defiantly. An unfamiliar feeling of pride washed over her. This would show a mortal just how futile any notion of attacking would be.

The double doors beneath her swung open and four soldiers marched in with a body splayed between them. Each fae carried a limb and the silver rope attached to it, thus affording little opportunity to escape. Reaching the foot of the dais, they stopped. Lana's heart started to pound. The man's head remained resolutely down however, hanging over the map.

Lana met the Captain's eyes. She flicked her finger slightly and he marched down the steps towards the man. She then flew directly above them and could see the man's reaction better. She wrinkled her nose - he appeared to have hairy snakes spurting from his head!

Once more the Captain checked with his Queen for her next order to be carried out. With the tip of his sword, he flicked off the covering on the man's head. The point then pushed under the man's chin, forcing it up to face the shining armour in front of him.

As one, the soldiers stepped forwards and pointed their spears at the prisoner.

Lana watched as the man grunted, then spat bloody spittle towards the threat. She frowned and dipped lower. Then the strange serpent ropes of hair on his head shook and he roared. A loud bellow of fury as he wrestled against the constraints on his limbs. She rose higher again - the fae holding the legs were clearly struggling against his powerful kicks.

"Why have you come to our lands?" Lana said imperiously as his noise abated.

A strange guttural language tore out of his mouth, finished with another growl of disapproval.

Lana began to see the problem Tolant had warned her about. Talking to him had been worth a try though, just in case Tolant had somehow not bothered with simple questioning. Verbal communication was going to be impossible if neither side understood what the other was saying. She flew closer to inspect him.

The man was tall, taller than any of her fae. His long legs were muscled and powerful, as were his arms. What had been clothing was loosely tied round his body, ripped in many places to expose bruised flesh. Tolant and his tools.

The silver ropes around his limbs looked secure enough, biting into his skin, leaving little red lines. He turned his head, as if sensing a presence above him. She had yet to see his face, but her curiosity was piqued. To the side of his head, his ear looked mangled. Half an ear? She wanted to reach out, touch it. Was the other the same? Was he some kind of half human? Usually unevenness made her feel slightly off kilter, but this fascinated her rather than repulsed.

She made a circle with her arm to the Captain. In unison, the soldiers closed in on the body. Swiftly swapping limbs, they rolled him then pulled apart. Before he knew what was happening, the prisoner was flipped to face upwards.

Lana was barely a body height above him. She narrowed her eyes and searched the man gaping up at her. Huge green wings flapped slowly, keeping her in a superior position. Their eyes met. Lana searched the depths of his vivid blueness. Sigurd froze, powerless to resist staring into her dark pools.

They studied each other for a long moment. Wrinkles on his forehead betrayed his years of living under pressure. She knew hers was as smooth as a washed pebble, straight and high. Mud and blood stained his skin, beard growth hid a firm jaw. Lana wondered what he was, underneath all the grime.

He assessed her pale skin, high cheekbones and narrow face, delicately framing the most seductive eyes he thought he had ever seen. As he tried to make sense of what she was, her slim curves suggesting a female, he understood immediately that she was not quite the same as the winged creatures which had brought him here.

The wings holding her aloft though...he could barely believe it. Was it some costume? A trick? Magic? Despite his immediate understanding that she had a human face, maybe even a woman's body underneath that lilac gown, nothing he had encountered before helped him to understand what was hanging over him.

Lana decided. He would not be a threat to her. Something about the fear she'd first read in his eyes had been tempered during their exchange to one of awe and wonder at her. Just a glimpse into his soul had revealed a conflict within, violence too, but not intentional. She felt a strange pull towards him, almost like a Lifeforce ribbon, but tangled. She breathed in through her nose... yes, a strange kind of Lifeforce. Not unpleasant at all. Not a threat. Besides, she knew her own capabilities better than he did. Should she so choose, he would be no more than a piece of skin wrapped around an empty skeleton.

Cautiously, she pointed at herself and said, "Lana, Queen of Naturae."

The giant below her nodded slightly, "Sigurd," he croaked. He was still unable to break from gazing at her. Lana felt a ripple beneath her skin as his eyes drifted again over her figure. Almost without realising it, she lowered and straightened up.

"Frigg?"

The guttural question made no sense to her. When he saw the flash of confusion on her face, she thought he looked relieved. Lana nodded at the guards holding his feet and gestured for them to release. He stumbled as his limbs suddenly hit the ground, finally breaking off the contact.

Pulling against the ropes holding his arms, Sigurd used the

leverage to get to his feet. He stood, cross-like with his long legs together, and looked once more at her. The intensity in his eyes made Lana suddenly conscious of her own pulsing heartbeat, faster and thumping stronger than it ever had. She breathed faster, as if she had recently exerted herself.

Lana tilted her head. A curtain of long black hair cascaded over her shoulder. The barbarian gasped. Flying closer, barely a few feet away from him, she noticed his breathing was also faster than she would have supposed of a human. Slowly she descended to the ground. Although shorter than him by some measure, she felt secure flanked by the two soldier fae still gripping the ropes which bound his legs.

She indicated an island on the map beneath their feet, "Naturae."

He studied the shapes intently. Sigurd had experienced rough maps before, scraped out onto bark or sand for guidance. This collage of different shaded wood outlined an extensive area unfamiliar to him. The faintly blue-stained outline he assumed was the sea, encircling islands. He examined silently for some moments, searching for a familiar rune or symbol to confirm, but found none.

Although he wasn't quite certain of the geography, he knew from navigating this latest voyage that they had travelled far west of his homelands. Whatever they encountered would not yet be drawn. Rognval was not the first Yarl to venture into this area. A few others had returned telling tales of rich lands across the Northern seas. Assuming these were the cluster of islands recently discovered with his brother, he nodded his understanding.

Then she removed the silver circlet from her head, showed it to him before replacing it. His eyes flared as he took in the delicate filigree metalwork. She smoothed her hair down as she said "Queen." Tilting her face up and looking down her nose, she pointed at him and moved her hand down.

The human immediately sank down to his knees. She smiled at the Captain in triumph. "See!"

Sigurd was still studying her attentively. "Bring me the vases," Lana said. A guard scurried behind the throne and returned bearing a tray of earthenware pots. Lana picked one up and poured the contents to the floor in front of him. She scrutinized his confused face for a reaction.

He glanced at the pile of silver pieces on the floor, forcing himself to keep his face neutral. He estimated many arm rings worth lay scattered across the wood. Rognval would have been happy. His heart thumped, heavy once more.

Then Lana emptied the next vase - a lesser quantity of gold clumped in tiny nuggets. She watched as he wrestled with himself, then met her eyes. She wasn't sure what she expected to see but it wasn't the sorrow she saw now. In the depths of his bright blue eyes, he did not betray a desire to have the gold.

The next vase contained nuts, berries and edible leaves. The side of his mouth tugged as he twigged what she was trying to understand. Nodding, because he hadn't eaten in quite some time, he relaxed a little into the game. A hunk of raw meat and the body of a fish followed the vegetation splatting to the floor. For a moment he wondered if she was taunting him, but after scanning her eyes, he saw only curiosity. He licked his lips, deliberately, enjoying her stare.

The next vase was more problematic. Blood splattered onto the floor, and his feet. From the way she tipped it out calmly, he knew she was expecting a reaction of some kind. Maybe something that would indicate his inner nature, his hugr? A measurement of himself as a warrior perhaps? He tried to temper his face. A brave Northman does not fear blood in battle.

Lana thought she saw his jaw push out, just slightly. It wasn't so much of a grimace, as resignation tinged with guilt. She inwardly marvelled at the emotions the humans played out through their faces, despite what they tried to hide. This was the first time she had been so near to one before, although she knew other fae had encountered them in much closer proximity.

Sigurd wondered whether he had done enough to persuade her of his needs and desires. She reached over for the final vase on the tray. As she tipped it, little pieces of translucent brown wings fluttered to the floor.

He frowned, then turned his head to study the soldiers around him. He pulled the cables holding his arms, as if trying to retract into himself. Realising, as the fear crept over him, they all had similar, although whole, wings. Beating steadily and calmly. His mouth dropped.

Lana rose, her face hardened and her wings - easily twice the size of the soldiers and a brilliant, beautiful green - held her mid air. Oh, but she was wondrous! Magnificent. Fearsome. He remained unconvinced as to if she was a creature or a god.

He broke off eye contact, and forced himself to stare down. If she was indeed a god, it was surely disrespectful to gawk. Although he had a certain amount of self belief, he also felt he was not worthy to be in the presence of this amazing power. His body had, at first, reacted to her as a man would to a woman, but she was so much more.

Lana read his fear. It was justified. The man was surrounded by fae who would snap him in two as quickly as she could click her fingers. They could drink him dry and leave only a husk. She knew the raw urges which drove worker fae, enabling them to hunt and survive. Impulses only tempered by training and tradition. Her soldiers were worker fae with combat training - they still needed to feed. How different would a human be to an animal, she wondered?

And yet, a part of her felt an unfamiliar desire to reach out and touch him. To gaze into his eyes and reassure that she would not hurt him. Inside, she questioned herself as to why she wouldn't though.

Curiosity. The thrill of the risk he posed. His strong muscles clearly more powerful than any one single fae, it had taken four of them to bring him under control.

There was more still. Something had passed between them. He had what she could only guess was an allure. Given that she had never been in such close proximity to a human before, did they all have this effect on fae-kind? Or was there something about this one that was affecting her? There was much she wished to know about this intriguing man.

Lana whirled away, "Take him back Beneath." She needed to gather her thoughts before she decided.

CHAPTER 9 – CONNECTION

They brought Sigurd raw meat, thrust through his doorway on a wooden platter. He tore into it, barely chewing before swallowing. The darkness of his cell hadn't allowed him to identify anything more, but the irony tang sat on his tongue as he waited. Wondering what would happen next. Perhaps that odd man with his sharp implements would revisit. He shuddered and clutched Thor's hammer through his dirty flax tunic.

Not long after he had licked the platter clean, the soldiers came. They loosened the cables from the rings on the walls and presented him with a bowl to relieve himself in. In the dim light of the moss-wick candle, he couldn't determine if these guards were the same as the others from yesterday's humiliation. They all looked the same.

Once more, they reeled in the ropes until he was splayed, then tipped him forwards to carry him down darkened passages. This time, because he had eaten and was recovering from the effects of the torture, he was more alert to his surroundings. The winged soldiers flew only a foot's length above the ground. Dark brown mud beneath him zipped past at an alarming rate. Then they emerged into a sunlit clearing.

Sigurd lifted his head and looked around as they moved, ascending trunks of the most enormous trees he had ever seen. His stomach lurched as they tugged him backwards, up and over a balustrade. He barely had time to register that they were going through tall double doors into some kind of circular chamber. The brightness of the day had a different quality there - diffused as if the sunlight was still battling for dominance. In places, patches of light chequered the pale wooden floor and the dust hovered in sunbeam shards.

There was a pause as they lingered outside another pair of doors. When this set swung open, pulled by unseen hands, they flew through into a room with a trunk at its centre. Darker here, Sigurd had a moment to quickly look around and down long corridors. There was the briefest of waits before they were off again. Sigurd recognised the polished floorboards of the hall he had previously been in. Where the strange goddess resided. His stomach clenched.

Brought up sharply to a halt, he felt the fingers clasping his wrists and ankles loosen. He landed ungracefully, face first on the floor with a thump. Despite the pain from being dropped, instinct kicked in. Twisting himself into a less vulnerable position, he breathed through the twinges in his joints and curled. Ready to spring up. To his surprise, the ropes slackened enough to allow him to rise to one knee.

Sigurd looked up, towards the dais, bracing to pounce. Flanked by only two soldiers, the Queen sat on her throne. A slight smile betrayed her amusement at his predicament. Even without the troops surrounding him, he recognized he could pose little threat to her. The four creatures retained his fastenings, and he knew they worked as one. At best, he figured he could topple two of them, maybe three, but that still left three winged warriors to overpower him.

He bowed his head in supplication instead.

"I trust you have fed now?" The Queen said.

Sigurd had no idea what she was saying, so kept his head down.

In the silence which followed, he was tempted to lift his head, meet those dark flashing eyes again. But common sense prevailed.

Cool fingers slid under his bushy chin and a tingle ran through his neck. His eyes rolled up, and he raised his head just enough to catch her gaze through his brow. She kept her hand there, not grasping, but gentle. Visually probing him. Her widening nostrils suggested she might even be inhaling him.

Oh Thor, he must smell bad! He jerked his face away and looked down again, uncomfortable with her assessment. The hand retracted.

Another voice said, "Highness, you should not get so close to him." Recognising the familiar tone of his torturer, Sigurd shrank back. There was reproach in the voice.

"He poses no threat to me, I told you. We have an accord." the Queen snapped. Sigurd understood her imperious tone and smiled. This goddess needed no man to tell her what to do.

He dared himself to peek up at her again. Pleading with his eyes, he relied upon her mercy to loosen the ropes which held him.

Seeing no guile in the vivid blue eyes, Lana gestured for the guards to soften the lengths. Tentatively, Sigurd stood.

Rather than meet her intrusive gaze again, he peered around the chamber.

He was less afraid or confused today, in the long, thin room, bright with sunlight streaming from high windows. Something about the space eased him. It took a moment for him to realise that the dimensions were not unlike the largest of the longhouses - the Great Halls - of home. Built to several stories tall, the chamber was airy and clean. Uncluttered by people, storage for winter, cattle and chattel. He admired the white branched arches which formed the structure for an ornately decorated ceiling.

Lana was scrutinizing him, he knew. Silently he absorbed and contemplated his surroundings. Sigurd deduced the ornate chamber proclaimed a long history. He noted the subtle sheen to the woodwork - many layers of polish meant much care had been lavished on maintaining this beautiful, calm place. He breathed deeply, forcing himself to relax.

Sigurd turned to the Queen and formed a cup with his hand. Lifting the imaginary vessel to his lips, he watched as comprehension spread over her face. "Water?"

"Cup? Drink?" Lana arched her eyebrow and turned to gesture one of her guards.

His torturer stepped forwards, sneering. "He does not deserve your kindness, Highness. You would do well to remember your purpose in bringing him here. Do not draw too close!"

The Queen ignored him and pointed at herself. "Queen Lana." She then pointed at him.

"Sigurd." His deep voice rumbled as he grew in

confidence.

"Sssegur?"

"Sigg-Uard," he enunciated.

"Sigurd," she confidently replied.

He smiled.

Water in a wooden goblet was presented which she passed to him with a raised eyebrow. His smile widened and he drank it - savouring the cool fresh taste in his somewhat gritty mouth. "Thank you." He dipped his head and stepped back a little.

She looked surprised, and he suppressed a chuckle. Didn't they have manners here? The man in shabby robes stood behind her tightened his lips. Sigurd then turned and pointed towards the clusters of islands on the map. "Nat...?"

"Naturae."

"Naturrrae...naturae," he rolled the word around his mouth. The Queen looked pleased. Bending down, he touched the blue lines. "Sea?"

"Mar," came the response, which he repeated. Then he started to walk across the chamber, pointing at things and saying his words for them. Repeating her reply, and watching carefully to check he had understood her meaning. Chairs, windows, floor, map, cup, clothes. They continued exchanging names for some time. Occasionally, he failed to wrap his tongue around the pronunciation. She would repeat it, slowing down the sounds to make sure he had them correctly, then blending them back together again.

When he ran out of definite objects, he began to mime activities. He had travelled to many lands and understood that a basic vocabulary of words began with identifying necessary items and needs, as well as the actioning words related to them. More than that, he had a natural aptitude for languages.

The Queen seemed to be enjoying the game, at times clapping her hands with eagerness to share the sounds and praise his correct pronunciation. The torturer remained resolute and stood on the dais, glowering.

Sigurd's mind was whirling. His movement around the room grew more confident and he dashed back and forth as he spotted another item to name. As the trust between himself and the Queen evolved, he felt the ropes slacken more. The soldiers holding them seemed to have mastered the art of fading into the background. He soon forgot they were even there to restrain him.

She reciprocated, flying to follow his long strides to point at things, emulating his arm movements to echo or clarify his descriptions. She started to add colour to the articles so that he might begin to build two or three word phrases. Using the map, with its patchwork of tinted inlaid shapes, he quickly picked up more than names.

He observed her face carefully to understand more about how she reacted to the hues. This only served to make him question his earlier definition of her. They shared an affinity for blue, purple and bright yellow. Both felt uncomfortable encountering red and orange.

As the afternoon wore on and the light outside faded, drab winged creatures slunk in with tall candles and placed them around the edges of the room. Soon the waxy scent of honey and fir reached his nostrils, and his stomach emitted an audible grumble. As she recovered from the shock he laughed, miming the act of eating followed by a grin of satisfaction. Rubbing his tummy for effect, her eyes glittered with amusement. Then he tested her by making a belching sound. His heart truly started to soften towards her, when in reply she giggled, then mimed a yawn and a stretch back at him. Any latent fear he had about her misunderstanding his joke was laid to rest.

He roared with laughter and nodded, "Yes, sleep!" She looked smug, her mouth slightly parted awaiting the next exchange. Sigurd noticed her small white teeth sat perfectly in pale pink lips. He couldn't help himself then, and leaned forward with twinkling eyes and blew her a kiss.

Her eyes flared. Like a deer startled by a nearby twig snapping, the casual flirtation seemed to confuse. She glanced at the torturer, as if seeking confirmation or clarification, but he had missed it. Bored by their antics, he had turned aside and was studying some scrolls in a far corner of the chamber.

Lana's gaze flicked back to his. He repeated the gesture, smiling encouragingly. Hesitant, the Queen pursed her lips and copied. As she blew, Sigurd reached out and grabbed the kiss from the air. Slapping it on his cheek, his grin broadened and he rolled his eyes in exaggerated ecstasy. Tapping his heart with his hands, he staggered around as a love-sick fool might.

Again, she seemed uncertain. He had been hoping to elicit a giggle. Since this had failed, he raised an eyebrow at her. Did they not have intimacy here? Even the gods know of love, of emotions, even if they didn't embrace them.

But then, was she a god? Her reaction to his earlier antics suggested she had feelings. Her excitement about sharing language had moved from caution to curiosity. He sensed a connection between them. In her eyes, he was also convinced he had seen some form of sympathy, and they had shared a common sense of humour. Sigurd was perplexed.

The Queen had clearly decided that enough time had been spent in his presence. She turned away and ordered the soldiers to tighten the ropes once more. His face fell, then grimaced as they yanked him into the star-shaped position once more.

He smiled at the floor, then tossed his dreadlocks to one side to see if she was watching him. Satisfied she was, he grinned, saying "I hope we meet again my Queen," over his shoulder. As they left, he heard the reproachful voice of the torturer, he hoped it wouldn't dissuade her from his company once more.

CHAPTER 10 – SILENT SUPPING

Lana forced herself to wait until the slivers of dawn light peeped through into her bedroom. The night had been long, and much of it spent pacing. She'd tried going to the Pupaetory and enacting her blessings to the vines, but somehow her restlessness prevented the flow of concentration. Her mind kept wandering back to the strange and intoxicating human.

Although she wasn't satisfied - in any way - that the cocoons had received sufficient, she'd given up and returned to her rooms. There was no joy in her duties since he'd arrived, and she found herself wanting to avoid her usual routines to explore these new feelings instead. Somehow. Anyhow.

Having abruptly drawn the last meeting with the alluring human to a close, her frustration grew as the hours ticked by. She had thought that some time alone would enable her to make sense of the sensations he provoked in her. Instead, a peculiar need for his presence had begun to override all logic. Turning over questions in her mind, walking the floors, was the only release she found.

In the depths of the quiet night, she replayed images, impressions she was forming of the human. How his brow furrowed in concentration when he formed her words. The creases in his cheeks as he smiled. And how infectious that deep booming laugh was - so much so that she couldn't keep herself from laughing as well.

The laughter - she tried to remember how long it had been since she'd laughed. It might have been before the Sation wars, some two centuries ago. Surely not? Had things really been that dull since then? Her mother, when alone in their quarters, had sometimes tried to break the tension of the situation by mimicking the Nobles at court. She'd had an uncanny ability to exaggerate their mannerisms, not unlike the gestures the human had used. She used to find the gentle mocking of her mother funny, although they never played that game in public.

Now, the hazy sunlight made its appearance through her windows, signalling a more respectable time of day, she hailed the guard outside her door and demanded to see the human once more. She wanted to see if he could make her laugh again.

*****

The soldiers carrying him in once again dropped him to the floor unceremoniously. The matted head of rope remained down for the briefest of moments. Then, he lifted and met her eyes. The vividness of them sent a jolt through her body. Her lips parted slightly.

But, he looked somehow less energised than yesterday. His face was paler, and breathing in, she realised his scent was lacking something. Without realising it, her face crumpled into concern. "What is wrong?" she said.

He seemed to understand her question. Rallying, he pulled against his ropes and manoeuvred himself into a sitting position. The guards slackened the restrains sufficiently and stood back to allow him space. He rubbed his eyes, then ran his hands over his face. The blood flow returned to his skin. He looked less flat, but his skin still had a grey tone.

Lana remembered that her mother had mentioned the humans need to rest. She too habitually laid on her bed and sometimes let her mind drift into another world during the dark hours. But in midwinter, the nights were longer. Perhaps human's needed to rest for longer then? Autumn and winter ceremonies were less lengthy, more intense. She hadn't considered it before. Had he not had sufficient recuperation time?

He looked at her again, then, coupled the gesture for a drink said, "Water." She couldn't help the broad smile spreading over her face. He remembered! Then he requested, "Food?"

Lana wheeled around, but her flank of guards was not yet present. She chided herself momentarily - of course they would perform in their requisite training time before the usual daily routine. It was very early in the day, far earlier than she would normally be present in the Hall. There were only the Beneath guards who had brought Sigurd here. She ordered, "Fetch a meal and water," to the nearest one.

The guard looked perplexed, so she curtly clarified. "Fetch one of the workers to serve meat or whatever you eat, and fresh water. There is no need for you to hunt, it doesn't need to be alive. Anything humans can eat will suffice." The soldier dropped his rope into a colleague's hands and scurried off.

Sigurd's full lips lifted at one side. He rose to his feet, somewhat unsteadily, waiting for her next command.

Lana felt her stomach shift - whether from his imposing height, or the way his eyes then roamed over her body, she wasn't sure.

The silence between them grew uncomfortable during the wait. Lana, finding herself at loss as to how to provoke their previous connection, turned and walked towards her throne. She blinked, frowning to herself without being able to identify quite why. She sat and arranged her gown neatly over her knees. Her wings fell into their usual place through the gaps at the back of the silver chair.

Rather than meet his piercing gaze, Lana allowed herself the luxury of roaming her own eyes over his body. As she took in the ragged long shirt he wore, mentally she stripped it from him and wondered at what his form might look like underneath it. His muscled legs were partially visible in between his fur lined footwear and the bottom of the brown tunic. She lingered on her examination of the curve of the muscles before moving her eyes up.

A bulge was twitching beneath the fabric around his hips. Her eyes darted up to meet his. She took a sharp breath when she realised he was gazing at her with that funny half smile. Something pulsed between them, almost like a ribbon of Lifeforce only stronger. Pulling at her own hips insistently. A flush rose up her cheeks.

She pulled her eyes away. Pushing her confusion to one side, she was relieved to see a worker enter. Lana tried to focus on slowing down her breathing as the tray was placed in front of him on the floor. Looking deliberately at the windows to the side, Lana heard him shuffle. From the corner of her eye, she waited as he picked up the platter and moved towards a chair.

She watched as he sat then began to stuff the food into his mouth. She studied his reactions to the items as he ate. A slight grimace as he tore off a hunk of what appeared to be a rabbit's hind leg. The fur still on it, he picked at it, then pulled the whole section of skin from it in a smooth manoeuvre. Rather than biting straight into it again, his fingers then peeled off sections before putting them in his mouth. He chewed for what seemed like an age then took a swill of the drink. Sigurd raised the joint to her and lifted an eyebrow.

"Rabbit," she said.

"Rrrabi," he rolled the word around, repeating it before taking another strand of the raw muscle between his lips. As he chewed, he put two fingers up on either side of his head and bobbed his torso a little. Lana smiled, "Rabbit."

"Rabbit," he replied as he finished chewing. "Good, tasty," he licked his lips and grinned back at her.

He left the berries until he had finished all of the meat. She named each berry for him before he put it into his mouth, identifying it by taste and learning. Savouring their sweetness, his shoulders relaxed.

Their naming game recommenced in earnest. Lana

commanded the workers to bring different animals into the High Hall, until an array of platters bore witness to his extended vocabulary. Squirrels, birds of many varieties, a small deer, mice, voles, fish. The day flew past.

Lana continued to be amazed at his ability to memorise their words. In the gaps between deliveries of new things to name, they began to delve deeper into her language. Attributing emotions to the animals, although it was harder with insects, and using their whole bodies to exaggeratedly mime personalities. A fox was cunning, a hunter. A fish somewhat stupid, swimming around aimlessly. A rabbit, swift and watchful. Acrobatic squirrels, nervous shy deer. A boar rooting for mushrooms, snuffly scavenging about on the floor made them both laugh.

As the workers came in to light the candles, Lana recognised their progress slowed. Having subtly fed from his energy all day, she found herself buoyed by their exchange and could quite easily have carried on all night. His movements were less extravagant now, although his eyes remained bright and alert, he was becoming depleted. Sigurd had snacked on plant foodstuffs as they went through the day, but it wasn't enough.

Watching him as he continued to try to think of new ways of opening up the right words to express himself, the pauses between visually identifying something lengthened. Lana understood innately that she needed to release him to rest. She turned away from him and frowned, struggled with the prospect. Her desire to be in his presence fought with her understanding that he required time apart from her to recover his Lifeforce. This was an everlasting and possibly dangerous battle, she realised now, one she would be fighting every moment he was with her. She had supped on him, and like the humans during the ceremonies, she thought she would recognise when enough had been taken.

Lana moved down the Hall, allowing herself time to process this revelation. She was satisfied in one way - the connection between them fulfilled more than her need for company, she realised. But it was not the same satisfaction which she derived from a ceremony. The Lifeforce gathered from the rituals was more akin to filling a well. It needed regular replenishment before she could - in measured doses - disperse energy as blessings to the lands and in the Pupaetory. This sensation of being complete in his presence was definitely not that kind of Lifeforce.

This felt more personal, as if it were just for her. And like a plant that can only grow in certain areas, she saw then that she liked that kind of enrichment.

Lana turned and studied him slumped in a chair. His breathing was shallow, his head motionless with his hair ropes touching his knees. Something in her wanted to reach over and push the snakes aside, touch him. But she recoiled inwardly, sensing that it would lead to danger. Had it been herself, tired and slow, her response would be to lash out. Push aside the intrusion.

Better to have him taken away. She didn't want to risk his rejection of her. Did not want to be so close to him that she would lose control of herself and pull yet more from him. With a wry smile of pride in herself at her self-discipline, she commanded the soldiers to return him to the Beneath.

As they tugged him to standing, he peered up at her. A glimpse of sadness in his eyes almost made her order them to stop. Instead, as they manoeuvred him into the transport position, she approached. The guards secured him face down then began moving. She flew over them to the doorway.

The procession paused. Returning to floor level, she bent down and cupped his chin, pulling it up for one last look at him. He was smiling, even though she could see his skin returned to a grey pallor. He dropped an eyelid down and back up again, and his grin broadened. The dark inner circles of his eyes grew so wide they almost encompassed the blue as they focused on her. Lana turned and flew out before he had the chance to react further. As she made her way to her chambers, her heart fluttered with joy.

CHAPTER 11 - REBELLION

This day, he had woken of his own volition. It made a change from being dragged, still half slumbering, out into the chilly earth tunnels. His eyes blinked as if that would clear the darkness from them. It was absolute in this empty hole he rested in. He wasn't even sure it was day. In the depths of...what had she called it? The Beneath or something...no light penetrated other than the thin wisps of the moss-wick and fish smelling candles they sometimes used.

He felt the earth underneath him, played with the dry dust. Lifting some to his nose, the smell of peat and decay prompted memories of the people he had been pulled away from. He wondered what had become of them. Presumably they were still there on the other islands, as he hadn't heard any other noises in theses depths. Had they been searching for him? Buried his personal items as if he were dead and shared out his clothes? Or just assumed he had wandered off, into trouble. It wouldn't be the first time he'd been inexplicably absent for a few days. But, he had always returned.

He cursed under his breath. His own impulses to explore, leaving others to settle or trade, they were to blame for his downfall. No-one was coming to look for him.

He found, as he turned this grim realisation about in his mind, that he wasn't especially bothered. The one person he had been closest to was gone. Whilst he had stood with the other men in battle, and latterly, leadership, he would be hard pushed to say he cared for them. It wasn't in his nature to be effusive - he watched their backs during fights because that was what kinsmen did. Stronger together.

And anyway, he reasoned, wasn't this situation the truest nature of going a-viking? Exploration, opening up new lands and opportunities? Smiling now, he realised that if he could return - how and when remained unclear - but he would return in triumph. With tales to tell of riches and strange other worldly creatures. Of palaces in immense trees. He almost laughed then - no-one would believe him! Maybe he would talk of them as gods. That might be more believable somehow.

His mind sank again, shoulders sagging with defeat. This fantasy would only be made real if he left. With evidence.

Sighing, he stood up and stretched. As he reached out his arms, his fingers touched the walls of the cell. Rising up onto tiptoes, his hands met the soil above. His heart pulsed faster. Confined spaces and he were never friends. He immediately yearned for escape. Not necessarily from Naturae, just this cell. There was much to understand on this island. In his heart, although he missed his kinsfolk, he was enjoying the utter strangeness of these...these...what were they exactly?

The more time Sigurd spent with Lana, the more confused he became. Sessions in the large chamber included food, for which he was grateful. He had no doubt that he enjoyed learning their language and the opportunity to study these creatures, especially their attractive Queen. But, when he was returned to his earthen cell, he was more tired than he believed could be possible. Yet more elated than a prisoner ought to be.

To make sense of it all, he needed further information. A greater understanding so that he could be clearer in his explanations of this place. He shuffled over to the wall, feeling with his fingertips for the door which was there somewhere. When his reach stopped, he used his foot. Leaning back, he kicked until the sound changed from dislodged pieces of soil falling, to a thud of wood. He kicked, stubbing his toe. The noise was satisfyingly loud in the quiet. Again, and again.

Then he waited. The aperture remained closed. So he thumped again. Switching position and leaning into the ropes for balance, he applied his other foot. Despite the pain in his shoulders from pulling against the restraints, he played a game with himself, alternating bangs and legs.

His desperation grew. Arm muscles screamed in protest, yet he still kept going. The beat echoed his thudding heart as he tried to double tap, one foot quickly followed by the other. The doorway did not budge. No-one came. Sigurd took a huge breath in, standing tall with both feet planted, and roared. The sound filled the small room. It felt good - alive. He filled his lungs once more. The next thunderous shout was even better.

Coursing through his body, the battle cry invigorated his every muscle. Primed for action. Sigurd pumped his fists and resumed kicking the door. Raining blow upon blow on the wood, he envisaged a shield wall in front of him. Brute force would overcome the enemy. Freedom beckoned.

*****

"The barbarian is beating down the Beneath!"

Tolant hadn't bothered to wait for an invitation before he barged into her chambers. Lana turned from her desk and glared at him.

"He should be removed. At once!" The adviser was practically shaking, fists clenched as he strode as if he owned the room to her desk. Lana couldn't remember the last occasion she had seen such colour in his face.

"He shall remain unharmed. He cannot get out," she said calmly, turning back to her papers. Her wings fluttered slightly. Tolant shifted around, bothering her eyeline.

"Your Highness, I cannot see how keeping him here, alive, benefits anyone."

"It's not about benefit, Lord Tolant." Lana sighed, already decided that it served no purpose trying to explain her confusing feelings about Sigurd to him. "It is my wish that he remain here."

"Having him here has not provided us with any information which we required." Tolant stuck out his lip, then changed his approach. "Your Highness, I can see that his presence provides you with amusement, but he is still just a human. No more, no less. Of no value."

"I think you are mistaken. We are making progress. And as Queen, it is my decision what to do with him, not yours."

Tolant grovelled, "I quite understand, and of course, it is

natural that you should exhibit curiosity about the mortals..."

He walked around the chamber, pushing his hands together. "But, that our Queen spends her valuable time toying with a human has not gone unnoticed." He looked sideways at her. "I am told the vines are in need of your blessing."

Lana shifted a little in her seat. She had been remiss in not visiting, she knew. "I will visit them today."

Tolant bowed his head to the side. "Your Highness, that is most gratifying to hear. I will inform the Pupaetory to prepare for your arrival."

He waited a moment, then pushed again. "Perhaps, your Highness, it would also be a good time to recall the Nobles to court?"

"Why?"

Tolant looked out to the trees and mists outside. "They might have some further news on the invaders to report. Who better to trust with the truth than our own kind?"

Lana brushed the quill over her lips as she thought. "No, not the Nobles. However, the spies possibly? They could provide some insight. That one from before, the one we went back to watch the lands the soldiers took him from. Surely by now he will have something to say about the invaders' reaction to Sigurd's absence. Maybe they have left?"

"I was just about to advise the very same, your Highness." Despite his platitude, Tolant glowered. Her familiarity with the daemon was perturbing. He refused to use his name, for even names carried power.

Lana warmed to the idea. "Maybe if I have some news of

his people, he will enlighten us with more detail on what they hope to accomplish."

Tolant frowned. "It does not settle the problem with the islanders, your Highness."

"What problem?" Lana was confused for a moment. Then she realised what Tolant was referring to.

"He is a leader. He could give us some ideas on how we can get the humans to return to the ritual. That would solve the issue, surely?"

Tolant looked unconvinced. "I fear you place too much faith in him. Has he given any inclination to divulge the secrets of his kind?"

"Secrets? He has no secrets! They are humans, as you said. They want something. We need to identify out what and give it to them. Then they will go away and things can return to normal."

In the silence which followed, Lana avoided looking directly at her irritating Advisor. At no point did she feel she was investing too much faith in Sigurd's capabilities. Surely someone who had such an intoxicating effect would be able to convince his own people to carry out his request. She watched herself clench her hands on her gown, just at the thought of him leaving, but felt unsure as to why the notion should give her such distress.

Tolant was not finished yet though. "Highness, forgive my impertinence, but if I may dare to venture…you are a Queen, and should not be expected to know the ways of humankind. This may mean that you are at risk of being misled about the extent of his cooperation and intelligence."

Tolant began to walk around the room again. Without realising it, the volume of his voice rose. "His behaviour doesn't inspire confidence. He shouts, he fights, he eats like a wild animal."

"He also has learnt to speak our language in a matter of days! Show me an animal which can achieve that!" Lana stood up, glaring at him. "That he needs to eat is a basic human requirement, however revolting we fae may find it."

"Your Highness! I just feel, you should not be consorting with... I merely meant to…"

She rounded her desk, her wings unfurling. "And yet, unlike you, he shows manners! He listens before speaking."

Tolant narrowed his lips but hung his head. Lana advanced on him, "Get out of my sight! How dare you infer that he is somehow beneath us."

"But," Tolant mumbled, "he is human. He *is* less."

Lana flew up and grabbed the collar of his robe, yanking it hard as she pulled him towards her face. "That just shows how little you understand, you fool!"

Tolant's eyes widened and he began to shake underneath his robes. His wings beat steadily to help keep him balanced upright. His gaze slid desperately towards the windows, avoiding her glare.

"But… he does not know our ways. Not like the islanders…" he muttered.

"This *isn't all about* the islanders," Lana snapped. "Without them, I *need* him."

There, she'd said it. Surprising even herself. Of course, she knew Tolant understood the role of the humans in ceremonies. Without their collective presence, there was no Lifeforce, and she could no longer bless. Few common worker fae fathomed this connection between ceremony and blessings, but he had been by her side long enough to figure it out. Only a royal could pull the ethereal ribbons then disperse them back into the ground.

What remained to be seen was whether Tolant would understand the effect this one particular human had on her.

Lana whirled away, dropping him. She needed to confirm for herself if just his Lifeforce was sufficient to enable her to perform her duties and grow the pupae. But, she hadn't seen Sigurd today. Better to see him first. Her heart beat faster and she moistened her lips. Maybe now he had more words he would be able to tell her what she wanted to know before she reached a decision on the matter.

"Recall the spies," she snapped before Tolant could object, and flew out.

Tolant stood for a moment, calming himself by surveying the ordered chambers. All seemed in place as it ought to be. He let out a long breath. Thankfully, the chaos the halfling's addictive blood could invoke had yet to manifest by altering her behaviour. But, the Queen's stubborn refusal to even entertain the future disposal of the human concerned him. Too much time spent in his company ran the risk of blood spilling and then, well, he didn't know the effect it would have on a royal, but he had witnessed the craze it caused for worker fae before. This halfling was unbalancing the situation more than he had expected, however. As he left, lips pinched together, he considered the options he had left.

CHAPTER 12 - STAKES

Sigurd had collapsed in a heap of exhaustion when the guards finally opened the door. With little strength left for resistance, by the time he was deposited in the High Hall, he had convinced himself that there was now nothing that could be gained by putting up a fight.

The Queen entered - graceful as always - followed by some of the servant creatures. He roused as he spotted the platters of food and gourds of water.

Lana appraised the man before her. He looked unharmed, although there was significantly more dirt on his clothes than before. He slumped a little, as though defeated. Smaller somehow. She lifted up his face, relieved to see the usual twinkling blues fizzle back at her, but the expression behind them? Submission maybe?

Her forehead wrinkled, unsure whether her assessment was correct. Then the sides of his mouth rose. Her body reacted of its own accord, flushing and tingling as his eyes roamed over her. The sense he had given up dissipated immediately. Lana couldn't help but feel relieved. Perhaps he would do more than cooperate today.

"Eat," she commanded, waving over the workers. As he tore into the meat, she talked. Knowing his language capabilities were still not as eloquent as she would like, she kept her request simple.

"Your people - you - have invaded our lands. You killed many people. I demand to know why? What do you want from us?"

Sigurd nodded, chewing as he decided how to answer.

"We come, from sea. Find new land."

"Why? What is wrong with yours?"

"It is what we..." He corrected himself, "I need to do. My land, different. Hard to grow. Hard to live. We need to go."

Lana frowned. "But why do you need to? Why kill? Why stop the people from doing what they usually do?"

Sigurd shrugged. "Not always kill. Sometimes trade. Sometimes take people. Get gold."

He thought of Rognval. There was no point in ignoring his desires in the list. "Some want gold. Land for family. For honour. To grow."

"Will more of you - men like you - come?"

Sigurd nodded. "In time."

She twisted away, heart sinking as she turned his assertion over in her mind. There were too many different wants for Naturae to ever accommodate. If it had been simply a matter of gold, that much she could have given. She could even apportion some of the islands to sustain them, or turn a blind eye to what they had already taken. But the fae could not openly defend the humans. Prevent the killing. They could not stop them without exposing themselves.

Sigurd put the platter down and stood. Reaching over, he touched her hand. She flinched and pulled it away, whirling around to confront him. His face fell as he saw tears welling up in her eyes. At that moment, he knew she was not a goddess.

"Why?" She whispered, "Why do you have to come?"

He looked down at her and gently wiped her cheek. "Because Northman nature." He shrugged, "Want go places. New places. New people..." He smiled. Lana's heart leapt. At the same time, she was disgusted with herself for reacting to him. The man, and all those like him, were dangerous. She had been a fool to think otherwise.

"You have no idea what you have done. How much damage your killing has wrought." Lana broke away from him. "You can never leave here."

A sense of shame washed over him. She was right. The manner of their arrival was brutal. "It will not stop others," he cautioned sadly.

She didn't want to believe him. However, she suspected he was telling the truth. Her hands curled into fists. There was little point in remaining here, trying to understand him and his ways. It would not prevent more of them from coming. She flew down the High Hall, blinking away the rising feeling of lost control.

Sigurd could not help himself, desperately he cried out to her retreating back, "Queen! I help you..."

She hesitated and turned to look at him. He held out his hand, reached out to her as he stood. Lana's heart flipped over in her chest.

Sigurd watched as she wavered, a wary look appearing in her eyes. It was not over yet.

"Queen," he began. "I want help." He nodded at the map,

his arm sweeping up beyond the borders of the sea. "Help know your....people. Then, tell my people."

Lana thought this was the last possible thing she wanted. More humans knowing of fae kind would be disastrous. She turned to the doors again.

"More understand, less Northmen come. I will tell."

She paused, not looking at him but allowing him to speak.

"They afraid of...'gud'. Not please the 'guder' to come, to their lands. These lands." He pointed at the picture, in case his meaning wasn't clear. "More men will not come," he said with growing conviction.

Her face crumpled in confusion. The word 'gud' was not known to her.

"Gud?" Lana turned, still hovering by the doors.

Sigurd struggled, the concept of faith was not one they had covered in their conversation thus far, so he had used his word for it. "It mean thing we..." he cast his eye around, searching for something, someway, to explain.

He picked up the platter, still with some food on it. Kneeling, he raised his arms high and chanted. Offered the foods to his gods. That he had something to offer at all added fervour to his prayers.

The words he sang sounded strange to Lana, although she understood immediately his intention. The islanders in the henge, or at other significant places across her domain, also sang during rituals. They did not bow like he did, but she had seen arms outstretched towards the skies. The ancient words the humans chanted were faelore made musical. A means by which the mortals released their Lifeforce to her.

Did that make her a 'gud'?

Flying back to hover in front of him, she searched his face once more as he paused in his adulation.

"Do you mean, if they think this is the land of 'gud', they will not come?"

Sigurd slowly nodded, holding her gaze as best he could in an effort to convince her. He had taken a big risky leap, he knew. But he could see no alternative to getting his freedom. And, watching her now, magnificent in flight before him, he questioned inwardly his earlier conviction that she might not be a god.

Lana alighted next to him. She could hear the blood rushing through his heart, beating furiously. Through narrowed eyes, she ascertained he believed this himself. As if urging her to believe in him, he took her hands in his. The heat of his fingers warmed her chilly hands. His skin felt rough, yet gentle. She wondered how she, a 'gud' felt to him. Should she be touchable? Were they real as she was? If he knew her, could he convince other humans to stay away?

She wrenched her hands back, and turned away from him. With a sigh, Lana caught sight of the leaves blowing on the trees outside. The green flutters echoed the feeling in her stomach - it was too much, these sensations he caused in her too overwhelming. And yet...

As she breathed, his peculiar Lifeforce taste tingled on her tongue. She closed her mouth and inhaled again - feeling the flourish of a ribbon entering her with a heady rush. The leaves rustled, tiny noises which her ears alone could understand, calling her. Then she remembered why she had brought him here, and turned to face him once more. She chewed on her lip slightly as she subtly pulled on his essence through her nose.

Sigurd watched her hands - wondering why the fingers were slightly splayed. He frowned, as he felt the tiredness creep over him. He blinked, then suppressed the sudden urge to yawn.

Lana noticed the tightening of his jaw however, and gestured to the guards to take him away. Without saying goodbye, she lifted up and left him there, bewildered.

CHAPTER 13 – FUNNY HOW IT ALWAYS COMES DOWN TO MAGIC

Lana couldn't concentrate as she tried to bless the vines. Her heart flipped every time she thought of his face, his hands, even his long legs. It was very distracting. Her mind kept coming back to one question. Could she trust him?

Once again, she placed her hands at the roots of the tall plants which filled the glass ceilinged room at the far end of the Pupaetory. Willing the Lifeforce to unfurl and dissolve into the soil. She focused on the encounter earlier, perhaps thinking more consciously about Sigurd would help. Their meeting had left her twitching, uncertain for once as to the way forward. Even though she had breathed in his complex Lifeforce, she wasn't sated. She wanted more.

But, her mind wandered to places where she found herself both reluctant and yearning to go. The gazes they shared rippled with energy, even more so when he touched her hands. Confirming his sincerity. Urging her to place her faith in him. She thought that might have been enough to produce the ribbons now. Within his Lifeforce, somehow, she had also sensed something different. She couldn't comprehend quite what, but it felt warmer inside, even more intoxicating than previously.

"Pah!" she burst out. It was no good. The heavy feeling in

the pit of her stomach was putting her off. He was putting her off. With his funny notions about 'gud'. She didn't feel like a 'gud'. She got the impression that a 'gud' might wield more power than she - whereas she herself had no magical way to solve the situation.

More men would come. They would take the humans. Take the land. Although, she wondered, if she stopped blessing the lands, would they stay? If they settled here, but the soil was barren, wouldn't they go away again?

With a sigh, she realised there was no other option but to try his suggestion. Before it was too late. She couldn't risk yet more of the humans under her domain dying and their ways being forgotten. Too many had already turned to the new faith flourishing on the mainland. She could not afford for it to spread to the local islands.

Furthermore, it could take too long for the invaders to realise the land here needed her blessings. By then, all that would be left of their rites - the ancient ways - would be destroyed. Forgotten.

Lana stood up, dusted down her dress. Habitually, she checked her crown before taking to the air. She flew down the line upon line of green stalked plants. A pang of sorrow hit her as she came to the ones nearest the exit. Here, the stunted growth of the cocoons hanging from the stems bore witness to her failure. She knew, just from looking at its withered brown outer skin, that the pupae inside would never breathe. It had received insufficient Lifeforce, a victim of her own negligence of late.

These innocent pupae too, were victims of the men from

the north. Their arrival was to blame for the lack of humans. She had attended the ceremony, but human numbers were too few. Lana pursed her lips, her mind made up.

*****

She ordered the removal of the ropes when he was dumped in front of her throne. Sigurd looked up at her, gratitude flushing his face.

"You may leave us," she commanded the guards as soon as they had unfastened the silver restraints. They hesitated. She flicked her hand at them, "Go!"

Alone with him, she flew off the dais and approached. Holding herself straight as she kept herself almost at floor level, she ignored the butterflies causing havoc within her. The fear of him was not due to the potential of him physical overpowering her, that much she knew.

"Thank you," Sigurd said. He rubbed his wrists and smiled at her from his knees. Dipping her head, Lana's lips turned up. She did appreciate his manners.

"What do you wish to know?" She asked. "To warn your people that they should stay away."

Sigurd looked at the floor, gathering himself. He had considered the likelihood of these questions whilst alone in his cell earlier. "What you are? What you can do. What magic you have."

Lana smirked, funny how it always came down to magic. And to think she once thought he too had magic. Now she realised it was just his effect on her. The secret of that made her tingle inside.

"We are Fae."

Sigurd waited for more. Lana stared hard at him, keeping her own face guarded and she assumed, regal. But his blank face showed he had no concept of what they were. How ancient and revered the fae were. A part of her rejoiced - the secretive nature of the fae had clearly worked, but now, she would be forced to reveal something, in order to save everything.

Sensing she needed to prove her powers rather than just tell him, she swept her arm towards the door in invitation. "Will you walk with me? I could show you our world, then you can tell the others." Her eyes sought confirmation that he would comply.

Sigurd let her lead the way.

Side by side, they strolled down corridors and past closed chambers. Sigurd occasionally caught a glimpse of a small winged creature flitting out of sight. The palace seemed enormous to him, hallways led into circular linking atria, from which further passages ran. Lana opened the door briefly to a room, and he snatched a peek at the activity within. Green and silver soldiers wielding shining silver weapons. The agility and force of the airborne fae made his mouth fall open in wonder. The chink of metal meeting metal resonated in his ears, but there was no accompanying cries of pain from fallen victims. Instead, the chinking sounded almost like chimes, but deadly in tone.

"These are just a few of the troops, doing their daily arms

practise," she said airily, pulling the Armoury door shut quickly. "There are hundreds more."

Moving away, and as he was processing the implications of an army of winged warriors, she opened the door to another room.

"We keep records here, marking our civilisation, our history."

She allowed him to stick his head through the aperture, even though it meant their bodies were distractingly close. He looked past the table in the centre of the dim room to where a trio of tall candles cast a cosy glow. He followed the square walls upwards, lined with shelves crammed with scrolls. The light from the candles didn't reach the top.

Sigurd said, "How do you mark?"

His question confused her until he made a scribbling motion with his hand as if drawing short lines.

"Faelore is written," she mimicked him, but altogether more elegantly flowing. "On vellum, with ink. I will show you another time."

She closed the door firmly, still not altogether trusting him. Tolant's words of caution rang in her ears, about his unpredictable violence. Their history was sacred, especially now all was threatened.

"We mark also," Sigurd said as they walked on, "but we mark everywhere!"

"And what do your marks say?"

"Everything - poems, ancestors, our kin." Sigurd began to grow animated, his arm waved as if to encompass the whole world. "Journey. Adventure! Tales." He laughed to himself.

"Even to mark where we were. That we were here."

"Your trail of dead humans does that sufficiently."

Although he didn't fully understand her words, her disparaging tone quelled his mirth instantly.

Having made their way out of the palace, Lana flew alongside Sigurd as he walked down the steps from the landing balcony. As he breathed deeply in, the scent of firs and flora became the smell of freedom. To Lana, the traces of Lifeforce emanating from him in a confusing jumble of colours persuaded her she was making the right decision. Here, in the open air, Sigurd straightened up and smiled.

As she alighted next to him, he tentatively took her hand. It felt warm, although the skin was rough. Lana decided now she was in control, that she quite liked it - touch linked them somehow, making her more inclined somehow to trust him.

He gazed across the clearing. All around, the tall trees seemed to whisper. The bloom of spring had passed and the summer light filtered through bright green leaves. He blinked, tipped his head back then it jerked forwards with a a powerful noise from his nose! Lana took a step backward. The loud shock of his sneeze was unfamiliar - for a moment she panicked that something was wrong with him.

Sigurd laughed and squeezed her hand. Lana blinked.

"Which way now?" He said, and the grin on his face reassured. She pulled him over towards a pathway leading behind the dark entrance to the Beneath. Her eyes flicked over to him as they ambled past the gaping hole in the ground. His grip on her hand tightened until it was beyond them, Sigurd's gaze resolutely forward.

Reaching a clearing, they approached an enormous pair of trees, mistletoe and vines creeping up the trunk and out onto the intertwining branches. Sigurd stopped and gazed. "What name of tree?" He asked.

Lana was surprised he, a human barbarian, had singled out these two trees - the most ancient in the land.

"This is Ash," she said, then moved to touch the second. "And Elm."

Sigurd's eyes flared, "Asker and Embla!"

Lana was sure she heard reverence in his tone. Then, he plucked two flowers from beside the pathway. He dropped her hand and gently placed the blooms on the sturdy exposed roots.

"These trees are older than I am," she said, pleased that he had somehow seen the importance of them to her. The ancient trees had been the focus around which Naturae had been built. Their strength was Naturae's strength, as long as they remained, so would their civilisation, it was told. This was true both figuratively and literally - the giant trunks supporting the citadel held grafts from these original trees, adding their vitality to the sacred structures above.

His smile when he turned back to her held an edge of nervousness. "Honour children of Yggrasil," he said.

Whilst frowning in confusion at his strange words again, it occurred to Lana, with relief, that he hadn't asked how old she was. Whilst she wanted to create a connection with him, as well as illustrate their differences, it was only the language barrier which had helped him not notice her slip up. Age was an issue she preferred not to expose. Who knew if his gods were ageless? Fae were close to immortal, even though worker fae had much shorter lives in general and aged faster than Nobles or herself. Royals could live until their bodies were literally stopped by unnatural causes. Her mother's death and the many who had fallen in the Sation wars were proof that they could be killed. It suited her not to reveal her immortality or vulnerability at the moment.

"Who are Asker and Embla?" Lana asked.

Sigurd smiled, "They parents of all. Gods."

"Like I am mother to all fae?"

Sigurd blinked. "You? Mother?"

"Yes."

His mind tried to process this. In his world, a mother was surrounded by her children. A mother cared for them, protected them. And yet he hadn't seen Lana show much emotion towards other fae. Or anyone, now he came to think of it. Except maybe him. She did have reactions to him.

His confusion was heightened by a niggling worry that he was in Mitgard. Was it possible that he had in fact been delivered to the land of the gods?

"Is Yggdrasil here?"

Lana shook her head, the word obviously important to him, but alien to her. "What is that?"

"Is big tree.... biggest?" Sigurd stretched out his arms, "Mother of all trees." He brought his hands together, wove his fingers into a lattice. "Link all worlds?"

Lana wrinkled her nose, "No, I do not think so."

Sigurd almost chuckled at his own stupidity. He couldn't

be in Mitgard. Or Valhalla. He distinctly remembered how he arrived here - and he hadn't died. Yet. It still didn't explain much of where they were, but he was convinced that this was an actual land. Not a place on another plane of existence. The legends he had grown up with were reasonably reliable in that regard; Valhalla awaited those who died well. His descendants were created from driftwood, Ash and Elm, from the great tree of Yggdrasil which connected the worlds of gods and darkness and death.

Sigurd let out the breath he had unconsciously been holding in. Lana touched his arm, "These are special trees to us, to Fae. But I am mother here, not them."

CHAPTER 14 - ANCIENT HISTORY

Lana and Sigurd stood together for a moment in the relative silence of the clearing, admiring the natural wildscape close by. Tall foxgloves with their pink columns of bells framed smaller orchids, peculiarly shaped flower heads nodding to the ground. Red and white campions clustered, the shadows of their leaves hiding tiny wild strawberry plants. The air hummed with insect activity.

Sigurd wrinkled his nose and indicated they had better move away from the pollen-rich area. He looked back at the ancient trees as they walked on, as if reluctant to leave their presence, but Lana had more she wanted to show him.

As they strolled Sigurd took her hand again, but said nothing. His mind was preoccupied with struggling to untangle what he knew, from what he saw. It didn't help that Lana's huge wings kept fluttering, touching his shoulders when they drew closer as the pathway narrowed.

Lana broke the silence between them with a question: "Why were you afraid of Mitgard?"

Sigurd looked at her with astonishment. His eyes darkened, had it been that obvious? He blinked, and then some part of him decided he had nothing to lose by being honest.

"Mitgard is..." he shivered, and mimed a shocked face.

"Surprise?" Lana prompted quickly. Happy that they were back on the familiar territory of him working to learn her language, she smiled broadly, not realising that this was at complete odds with the concept he was trying to portray to her.

He frowned, he could only convey how he felt about it as there were no real known specifics. Only legends. Also, he hadn't really covered feeling words as yet with her. He thought, then picked a flower from a nearby bush.

"Dog rose?" Lana looked totally bemused. Then he smelt it and smiled, pointing at his grin.

"Happy?" Lana was confident that was the word he wished to know.

He pricked his finger deliberately and winced.

"Hurt?"

Then he pulled his lips down, threw the flower to the ground and mimed bereft.

Lana was not sure if he meant sad or how she felt sometimes, heart-sick. "Unhappy?" She waved her hands over the mass of flowers on the bush then pointed at his singular one. "Lonely?"

Sigurd grasped her concept immediately. He picked another bloom and gave it to her with a smile. She took it gingerly, avoiding the thorny stem with slim fingers. "Not lonely," he said as the wrinkles on the side of his eyes creased. He still needed to explain the right word though.

Her eyes grew wide as he glanced at the flower, then crushed it in his palm. Then, he placed the remnants on the soil beneath them and covered it with earth. With his hands he created a bird like shape and fluttered his fingers away from the grave.

"Death?"

He nodded, then raised his eyebrow and twisted his face with puzzlement.

"Unknown?" Lana wasn't convinced this was right. He repeated the sequence of death and flight but changed his direction of travel, ending with a bemused face. Lana studied his body, searching for clues there. His stance was lent slightly back, and he had left his hands somewhat claw like. "Fear of unknown?"

"Fear!" Sigurd's face immediately transformed as she made the connection he sought.

"Mitgard is frightening because it is unknown?" Lana confirmed.

"Yes!"

She grinned happily up at him, pleased with herself for finally giving him the word he sought. A thought then occurred to her, "Naturae, and the other land you came to, they are not known to you though? Why were you not afraid to go there?"

Sigurd chuckled, "They can reach by sea, not unknown. Tales told of lands come back to us. We know rich lands here and not need death to get to."

Lana began to understand. It re-enforced her earlier decision that he would need to return to the lands to speak of theirs and warn people away from it. However, simultaneously, to reveal Naturae would demystify it.

"Do you not fear unknown?" Sigurd asked. "Fear death?"

"No," Lana said, "And yes." She paused in their walking. "Usually, fae do not die."

Sigurd saw a flash of pain across her face when she had said yes, and he squeezed her hand gently.

Lana took a breath in and haltingly said, "Royalty lives forever, unless our bodies are killed."

This sort of made sense to Sigurd, gods do not die because they exist in another place. If they can be killed, she was not a god after all. Perhaps the fae were something in between.

"When we die, if we die well, we go to Valhalla. Be with family before us. Is not place of fear, but of happy," Sigurd said.

She smiled, "That sounds good. Where is Valhalla? What is it?"

Sigurd responded with his best description, "Big hall of warriors, eat food - boar!" He grinned, having remembered the word for the hairy pig which had been produced when he had first started to learn her vocabulary. "God - Odin - on big chair. Drink. Laugh. Happy. Friends and family, all there."

He felt a pang just thinking about it. Rognval would be waiting for him. And his mother, father and sister.

Lana frowned as his expression fell. Why was there now sadness when he spoke of this place?

"Who is there, for you?"

Sigurd looked deep into her eyes, surprised that she had read him so well. "My brother, Rognval," he said. "My mother, the shield maiden Shiorria. My father, Yarl before Rognval. My sister, a child who chased me until I could run no more." As he reeled off their names, their faces flashed before him. His shoulders dropped and he stopped to lean against a tree for a moment. His hand automatically reached up and fondled his hammer.

Lana tasted the wispy ribbons emanating from him. They were bitter, sour somehow. Their fragility touched her, and made her feel his sorrows. It wasn't pleasant, reminding her of the last sight she had of her own mother.

"We do not pass to Valhalla when we die." She said, trying to distract him from his memories, which left an odd sensation deep within her. "Fae re-join the light when we expire. When my mother was killed, the essence of her just...floated away. I think maybe she became part of the mists. Like ribbons dissolving."

It didn't make a lot of sense to Sigurd, but he appreciated that she was sharing something personal with him, even if he couldn't understand all the words she used. He was still feeling a little vulnerable; it looked as if she might be also. He pulled gently on her hand, bringing her closer to him as he leant back against the tree. She copied him. They stood side by side, both gathering strength from the wood. Leaning into the bark, their fingers each touched its rough warmth as they silently mourned.

Sigurd was reminded of a time just after his sister had died. His mother, worried about his retreat into the forests alone in the weeks which followed, had found him. Despite him not wishing to engage with anyone, she had searched until she saw him curled up at the base of a huge fir tree. Unreachable. But his mother had managed it.

Wary but wanting to connect with Lana somehow, he

reached his hand over and stroked the back of her hand with just one finger. Her eyes darted to his. She pulled her hand away from the curiously intimate gesture.

"Why did you do that?" She said.

Sigurd shrugged, "I need to."

Lana frowned. The word need implied so much more than she had intended to instigate with him. She hardly recognised the scope of the emotions which this curious man prompted within herself. This slight touch was yet more that she didn't know how to react to. And yet...perhaps it had been what she needed also?

"I do not need it." She pushed him away, but her eyes slid back to watch his reaction.

He just looked at her, and they both knew she was lying. He moved from the tree and walked casually up the path. She reluctantly caught up with him.

CHAPTER 15 – SHIFTING SANDS

The narrow track led Lana and Sigurd through denser forest, green and fragrant. The sunlight strained to reach the ground in parts. Sigurd noticed the trunks grew mossier the further they walked in the stillness. Woodland birds cried out as they broke twigs and snapped ferns to follow the pathway.

Sigurd joked about flying being faster, but they fell into a comfortable silence thereafter. He began to lose his sense of time. Usually he would use the position of the sun as a guide, but the canopy obscured his view.

He wanted to ask where they were heading, but then they hit a wall of mist. She carried on, pulling him into the thick fog until it enveloped them.

Sigurd paused, jerking Lana to turn and face him. He looked over her shoulder at the shimmering grey. He could barely see beyond an arm's length behind her. The dampness began to pervade his clothes and he felt a chill where it touched bare skin. It was unlike any fog he had ever been in, both in density and colour. It was like being inside a cloud, he thought. When you waved an arm through it, the glistening droplets sort of parted then reformed around the limb, as if eating it.

"Is this your magic?"

Lana nodded slightly. She couldn't explain how the

ancients had woven the mist millennia ago. Her eyes watchful, she said, "We, Naturae, cannot be seen. The mist protects the whole island."

Sigurd sniffed the air, noticing now a faint smell of seaweed. They had arrived close to a shoreline. "From sea, cannot be found?" Sigurd felt stupid even asking, but he was beginning to understand how they had sailed right past. A thick mist could hide unknown dangers as well as interfering with navigation. Wise sailors would circumvent it entirely if they could.

Lana smiled. Even through the haze, he could see her perfect white teeth.

"You cannot find us, no. But perhaps you would not try if you knew?"

Sigurd thought for a moment. Too many tales had already made their way back to his homelands to discourage Northmen from trying to reach far-away island shores.

"What word for...?" He waved his hand through the cloud.

"Mist."

"You make mist on other islands too?"

Lana shook her head. "Just where Fae live."

He turned away. "I not see how to stop people from going to other islands."

Lana reached out and touched his face. It was peculiar to feel the stubble of a man's chin, softer than she expected. The knot in her stomach had to be resolved though. "What must I do to stop them, then?"

The gentle pleading in her voice cause the ache in his heart to intensify. He couldn't see what he could do to help her. He gazed down into her dark eyes and felt the crushing responsibility she bore. They were not gods, even if they had magic. "Why are you worried about the people on the other islands?"

Lana took a deep breath in, then chewed on her lip a little. He smiled, thinking the gesture was far too human. Watching her mouth however, he could not help but think about other things he wanted to do with those lips.

"They need to attend the ceremonies."

Sigurd frowned, "What is...?"

Lana dropped to her knees and mimed the same ritual that he had used to explain the concept of gods. She stopped, "Ceremony. It is needed for...us? For the good of everyone."

His brows didn't release his frown. He looked down at the Queen. He knew gods demanded worship, hadn't he too paid homage to his gods? But she had used a word he understood to mean more than a desire. A need. Gods needed no-one. However, they would only bestow favour on those who honoured them.

Lana stood and smoothed her gown. She turned to walk back but stopped, and looked sadly at him. Sigurd realised that god or not, he felt a need to honour her. More than that, he acknowledged as his groin grew tight looking at her slim body, he wanted to in a great many ways.

Sigurd turned to face the gentle breeze, which didn't shift the mist at all somehow, but could be felt as a chill on his cheeks. "Can we see the sea?" He asked.

Weighing up the chances of his escape, Lana agreed. She carried on through the mists, with Sigurd keeping close behind her as the path narrowed. Before too long, he could feel the shifting surface of sand underneath his feet. He couldn't see much beyond her green wings, so with a lengthy stride, he caught up with her, catching her hand as she walked.

They paused after a few more steps, hearing the crash of waves and the rattle of pebbles being pulled back. Raising an eyebrow, Lana said, "Do you want to go further?"

Sigurd continued on in answer. The temptation of the water was also a comfort. Although he couldn't see where the waves were, he felt compelled to touch it. Deeper sand made his footing unstable. So he sat, pulled off his woollen socks and boots, and wriggled his toes. With Lana close behind him, he strode off with greater confidence, mentally measuring the distance to the waves by sound and saturation of the sand.

Lana hung back a little as he reached the rippled area where footprints quickly filled with water. Although her bare feet weren't cold, she disliked the sensation of granules of sand on them. She rose into the air to follow him instead.

Reaching the shallows, Sigurd tilted his head upwards and felt the cool sea air refresh the skin on his neck. Although he missed being able to see the vista of the ocean, just getting his feet wet connected him with home.

"Do you swim?" Lana asked curiously, noting the satisfaction on his face as he stood there. He looked strange with submerged legs, as if he had been cut down to size. Somehow more like the humans she had watched from above in the henge. Even those odd hair ropes seemed more appropriate for their location.

Sigurd raised his eyebrow at her, and she briskly paddled her arms and legs. With the sight of her - suspended mid-air by flapping wings, limbs furiously pumping - Sigurd smiled as he mimicked her motions. "Swim!" He laughed, "Yes." He bent down and scooped up a handful of water. He sprayed it over his face, then shook his head, laughing again.

For a moment, Lana wasn't sure if she ought to be offended by his parody of her. The fizzle between their eyes reassured her. Then he grinned and crouched low in the shallow waves. Sigurd began to scoop the brine over himself. Rubbing the grime from his face, his hands, and arms before rinsing. He pulled off his tattered outer fur jacket and tossed it back over to the beach. Before long, his undertunic was almost completely soaked.

Lana hovered, initially curious at the man's washing routine, then, when it seemed he had washed everywhere, he looked up at her. Presented himself with clothes clinging to his wet body, arms open and his palms faced forwards, as if awaiting judgement. Lana pretended to frown, but the slight tilt of her mouth gave her away.

Sigurd held up a finger, pausing her. Then he lifted a knee, and made a big fuss cleaning in-between his toes! Sticking his tongue out of the side of his lips as he balanced on one limb, diligently checking they were suitably cleansed for her. Lana stifled a laugh then flew closer, remembering the fond tone in his voice when he talked of his sister. She knew how sibling fae played together when they were young.

He froze, one leg up still, and looked at her, his eyebrows

wide. Had he done something wrong with his jokes? Before he could get his balance with both feet, she flashed a grin at him, then shoved his shoulder. Over he tipped, back into the waves!

Sigurd burst into laughter. He shook the water from his face and gathered himself onto all fours, still howling. He was absolutely delighted that she had joined in with his game - bettered him even!

Lana was thrilled with herself also. She giggled then flew just out of reach and sight, hoping he would take the bait. He did. Lurching out of the sea, he splashed over towards her direction of travel, reaching up as if to grab her. Then theatrically fell into the water as she darted away. Lana couldn't help laughing. She appeared to him again, deliberately close enough so that he would be able to see her feet.

Again, he tried to capture her ankles, but she pulled her legs up. Down into the water he splashed. The next time, he consciously sprayed the chilly sea higher. Shrieking as the cold hit her, she flew up and out of his way. Never going too far away, even though the salty taste in her mouth was unpleasant. She kept close, sometimes pushing him from behind then darting away, but always near enough that he could find her through the mist. They played cat-and-mouse splash until Sigurd capitulated.

"I not catch you, Queen," he panted. He staggered out of the sea and collapsed on the beach.

Lana felt as if she were glowing - she couldn't stop grinning. No-one had ever challenged her, or liberated her, like he did. She didn't care for once that her hair was messy, and crown slightly askew. She set down on the sand next to him. They caught their breath for a moment, calmed by the lapping waves.

Sigurd picked up a pebble, turned it over in his hands. Pale triangular shaped sandstone with two longer sides and one short, it fit neatly into his palm. He leaned over and drew two parallel lines in the sand. Then, he added a cross in between the top, linking the two marks with tiny triangles. Turning to Lana, he said "Man." Gesturing to the lines, he added, "Human."

Lana smiled and took the stone from his hand. She drew a swirl in the sand, a spiral almost like a snail's shell. Adding two curly notches to the top of the shape, she said, "Fae." Then she wrote the symbols for her name, and pointed at herself. With a wink, he added a crude triangle on top of the symbol, and pointed at her crown. Lana felt her cheeks flush as their eyes met with a now familiar fizzle between them.

He grinned broadly and began to draw other runes into the sand. As soon as he identified the fae word he knew - or could mime it - underneath his lines, Lana transcribed the equivalent name. Or, as close as she could understand them to be in Faelore. The extension of their learning game excited them both, and before long, the tide line where the sand was most firm was littered with footprints and signs. Writing re-enforced Sigurd's recall of the words he was already committing to memory. His unique mind created links and absorbed the pattern of the language without conscious effort.

Lowering levels of summer light filtered through the mist

as the sun began to think about setting. Gulls gathered, calling for them to vacate their beach so they could fish in the rising shallows. Lana noticed and guiltily realised that they had been out for almost the entire day. Not once had she attended to her daily duties, or even thought about them. Time slipped by so quickly with this man. He commanded her attention fully, which was simultaneously wonderful and worrying.

Resolved to do better the next day, Lana saw that Sigurd had also paused tracing in the sand. He turned to her, twisting his upper body whilst his feet were planted, sinking in the soft wet surface. "By tomorrow, they will wash. Wave take away." The regret in his voice touched her.

"We can make more marks," she encouraged. She too suddenly yearned for some semblance that this encounter was permanent.

Sigurd's head lowered, and he scanned the scratches in the sand once more. "One more time," he said, and began reciting the lists of words and symbols. The tide chased at their heels, washing away the marks and evidence of their exchange. Hand in hand, the couple walked back up the beach and into the forest again.

CHAPTER 16 - NECESSARY CHANGES

The Captain hadn't really known what to make of his Queen and the former prisoner when they arrived at his rooms at the base of the majestic citadel trees. "The human requires sustenance," Lana ordered as soon as he pulled open the door. Lana then glared at her companion, trying to quieten the grey looking but still cheerful Sigurd - still chuckling to himself and completely oblivious about the correct behavioural code when she was speaking to subordinates. She mentally shrugged aside her concerns about how she herself appeared and stuck out her chin, drawing herself up as if nothing at all was remiss. Bedraggled and still slightly damp - the Captain had loyally not even twinged a mouth muscle as he looked them over. Being Queen had some privileges.

Although taken by surprise at the demand, the Captain said he would seek advice on the matter of human meals. Meat could be provided with due haste. He shook his head to himself as they left. Presumably because he was not usually asked to supply food for a mortal, Lana decided. Well, all those in contact with Sigurd would have to get used to it. Humans apparently needed to eat frequently. She ordered the meal be brought to the ante-chamber in the High Hall.

Two young soldier-fae hurried after them as the couple skirted the sides of the clearing. For now, the knowledge of

Sigurd's freedom was best known to as few fae as possible. Hidden by the structures above, anyone flying would be less likely to spot their Queen and her human companion. As they climbed the stairs to the landing balcony together, Lana felt herself tense nonetheless. Then, without warning, Sigurd stood at the edge of the platform and started to serenade her! She recognised the tune - he had already sung it to her as they made their way back through the forest. Lana's eyes darted to the guards. Open-mouthed, they were unsure what to make of the spectacle - as would be any fae who was working in the vicinity, Lana realised.

She surprised herself further by having to suppress a small giggle, but she felt her cheeks flush regardless. Sigurd had, whilst they were in the forest earlier and in a faltering tongue, tried to explain how some of the words to the song had double meanings. The language he used coupled with his explanatory gestures, had left her puzzled. Faelore had no equivalent, which seemed to cause him mirth. Demonstrating these peculiar movements only highlighted his difference.

As he was entirely unabashed as he performed and didn't appear to be aware of the strange looks he was now attracting, Lana tugged on his arm. She tried to shush him. But, Sigurd continued - louder if it was possible. He saw her distress, and it seemed to amuse him. At that moment, she realised that were he to understand her intentions of keeping him hidden - the greater the chance he would rebel and become even more vocal. Briefly she regretted loosening his ropes earlier that day.

Had it been anyone else, Lana knew she would have had

them slung in the Beneath for their disrespect. He was different though. It excited her a little that he wouldn't take orders, even from her. No-one had ever challenged her thus. Even his laughter - she somehow knew the intention was not to embarrass her, or defy her, but to encourage her. She appreciated the performance was entirely for her benefit alone.

The problem was, she liked the person he seemed to think she was. The one he brought out in her. The one who laughed, and felt. But that was not the Queen of Naturae.

Ambivalent about how to manage the situation, Lana turned and flew through to the High Hall. She glanced behind and saw he had quickly followed once his audience had disappeared. Smiling to herself, she showed him into the ante-chamber. The guards arrived, and she closed the door on them all without saying a word.

*****

Having torn herself away from Sigurd, Lana dipped and whirled for a moment in the High Hall. She shot her throne guilty glances. Still giddy from the hours she had enjoyed - yes, enjoyed - in his presence, her body tingled, as it did after a successful ceremony. She was desperate to see if this sensation could prove an alternative to the ceremonial Lifeforce. Although she thought Sigurd now understood there would be no escaping the island, the guards would stay watch outside the door whilst he ate. She wanted to try again at the Pupaetory.

Unfortunately, Tolant had seen them returning. Still in his tatty robes, he was lurking outside in the inner atrium for her. Her happiness was short-lived, ruined by the advisor's glare.

"The Captain tells me the barbarian has become a guest?" He said snidely. "You should have guards with you, I fear you have placed too much trust in him. Your Highness," he added.

"Lord Tolant, I will do as I please. I am Queen."

"Of course," he bowed. "I am, as ever, only thinking of your safety."

"I am quite safe enough."

"And how are things in the Pupaetory?" He fell into place behind her as she flew down the hallway. Lana rolled her eyes, thankful he couldn't see the expression on her face.

"Quite well," she said lightly. "I will be returning momentarily."

"I have had word that the spy has returned. I looked for you there earlier..."

Lana stopped. "Have him brought to my chambers. I require a change of gown before I go back to the Pupaetory. He can wait outside until I am ready."

"Naturally, I thought you would want to know as soon as possible." Tolant's face twisted. "Wouldn't you rather receive the spy in the High Hall, as custom dictates?"

She frowned, "I know my own mind, Lord Tolant." And she couldn't rely on Sigurd keeping quiet.

"Do you, your Highness?"

Confusion flashed across her face and she wavered for a moment.

He continued, "Perhaps you think the invaders' appearance means we should abandon all of our customs now?" Tolant saw a shift in her eyes. But it didn't stop him - she didn't appear to grasp the danger from the halfling's continued presence.

"Or is it that your barbarian might make his own mind up about which ways we keep, and which we lose? Maybe you should ask him. After all, he has a royal at his level, showing him around."

She studied him silently, gritting her teeth to hold back the retort.

Misreading her silence, Tolant said sarcastically, "Are there any secrets which you *are* prepared to keep from him?"

Lana flew at him, not concerned that her stronger wings would crush his against the wooden corridor. Pinning his slight form to the wall, she hissed, "What I choose to impart to the human is my concern, not yours!" Dropping her grip on his shoulders, he slid to the floor but his eyes still glittered up at her with malice.

"You have spent too much time in his presence, taken on his violent traits." He sneered, the knowledge of what had already been put into play emboldening him. Now he needed his Queen to see the light - goading her was a risk but the only way. "Perhaps he will take over your mind next."

Lana gasped, the impudence of man!

"Or your Queendom..." Tolant's face twisted.

"Get out! Get away from me!" Lana's roar reverberated through the passages. In the distance, a clatter of dropped platters and weapons could be heard.

Lana could feel her face flushed with anger as she hovered above the wretch. Tolant turned to his knees and crawled away from her wingspan. Then he flew, very fast, down the hallway. Out of her sight.

CHAPTER 17 - LEAVES

The spy stood in front of Lana, quaking. In the royal bed-chambers - not a room he had ever been in before or would be again - he reported what he knew.

"They argue a lot," he mumbled. "Over what seems to be the strangest things. They fight between themselves, sometimes drawing blood. Some invaders have started living in the stone homes. They do not allow the humans out of their sight. Their boats stay on the beaches."

Lana had been listening, wondering how much of this information she could tell Sigurd. Then she asked, "Have you seen anything which might indicate they are leaving again?"

Issam shook his head, his brown wispy hair hung around his face, masking it.

"What of the Nobles? Have you found them?"

"My Lord Tolant told me they were to remain in hiding except for ceremonies. I do not know where they are." Issam's head sunk even further into his chest. The interrogation did nothing to ease his sense of failure.

"Have any more barbarian men arrived?"

"No, your Highness. Not that I have seen."

"And what of their behaviour since we took one of them, any change?"

Issam screwed up his face. It had been over a week and he

was hard pushed to think of much which had been different to his observations prior to the snatch. "Not obviously, your Highness."

Lana thought, perhaps Sigurd wasn't as important to them as she had at first been led to believe. She sighed.

"He - the one the soldiers took - was definitely the human who seemed to be telling the rest what to do." Issam tried to save face. "Maybe...yes, I think there have been probably more fights between the invaders since he was taken."

He nodded, more to himself than to the Queen. "Oh yes, there was another one who was trying to get the others to sail away." Did she really want to know the day-to-day occurrences of the village?

Lana sat up. "What was he like, the invader who wanted to leave?"

"Oh. Um...tall? Red hair? He took a lot of the weaponry and loaded them into a ship before the other people stopped him. There was another fight then, which he won, but he didn't try and go again. He has a big sword, very powerful."

Issam continued as Lana watched him with her full attention. "Weapons seem very important to them. They clean them and sharpen them all the time when the islanders are watching. Yes, weapons are special to them. And food. And drink…"

The Queen must have realised he was babbling. She had however, stopped grilling him, so after a pause, Issam said quietly, "I have nothing else to report, your Highness."

Mulling the information, Lana dismissed the spy and started to pace. She considered sending for Sigurd, to ask who the red-haired man was. What his intentions might have been. Then she realised that she was really just looking for reasons to see Sigurd again. She would go to him - safer that way. The Pupaetory could wait, she was sure this would be a brief visit. Just to check he had eaten. Maybe recovered a little. That was all. Enroute to perform her duties, nothing remarkable about that.

****

As soon as Lana flew through the door to the High Hall, she knew something was wrong. All thoughts of asking Sigurd about the red-haired man disappeared. Several worker fae clustered around the small chamber where Sigurd was supposed to be. Slowing as she reached the doorway, the workers dispersed in a flurry of brown wings and tunics. The guards she had left outside were nowhere to be seen. An older fae hurried out, whipping off a mottled apron and bundling it under her arm. Another followed, carrying a wooden bowl. Lana approached and they stopped dead in their tracks.

She searched their faces. Fear. Guilt maybe? Confusion.

"What is going on?"

The female fae dropped their heads and bobbed in synchronisation. Lana looked beyond them, through the doorway, whilst hovering for their reply. All she could see through the half open aperture was the green and silver backs of the guards. The workers glanced at each other, then the elder piped up, "The human, your Highness. He's been taken poorly."

Lana glanced down at the bowl, the acidic smell finally registering. Mottled greens and browns, with streaks of blood, identified the contents. Food remnants which can only have come from a human.

A young-looking guard turned and flew towards her, a panicked expression on his face. He stopped short, then awaited her invitation to speak. Lana nodded and the words spewed from his mouth.

"Your Highness, the prisoner was fine! He ate all the food. Then he started making noises and…" The young guard shook his head, not knowing how much to describe of the violent retching he had witnessed.

"And what?" Lana clenched her fist. Really, those from the last good-growing batch of pupae were stupid.

"His food reappeared! From his mouth!"

Lana's face fell. The soldier attempted to plaster over his own look of horror with a guise of competence.

Thinking quickly, Lana turned to the female workers. "Could it be something he ate? What did you bring him?"

The younger of the two, began to shake. Her brown hair had come out of its tie and fallen, hiding her face.

"Well?" Demanded Lana. She nodded to the guard, who immediately flicked his sword under the fae's chin, bringing wary eyes up to meet Lana's.

"We only brought the food which the Captain ordered us to take," the older fae interrupted, pushing her shoulders back and standing taller. "The meat platter, leaves and berries which had been gathered, as instructed."

There was a loud groan from the chamber, distracting

Lana from further debate about who was to blame. She turned to the guard, who offered up, "He is on the floor, your Highness. Writhing. May we put the ropes back on?"

Lana thought quickly. Knowing now how much his freedom had helped to restore him, she shook her head. "Just make sure he doesn't leave the room, or die here!"

Then she gestured to the females and ordered them to fetch the Lord Protector. No-one knew more about the plants and animals on the island than he did, much as though it annoyed her to even ask. "Find him! Quickly."

The guard re-entered the chamber, leaving Lana to pace the High Hall alone. A part of her yearned to see him, fearful it might be for the last time. But she could not risk herself, there was no other to take her place. Sigurd was too unpredictable and only two guards were in there to protect her. The knot in her stomach intensified with every groan that came from the doorway.

*****

By the time Tolant strolled in with no sense of the urgency which Lana was feeling, the antechamber had fallen silent. Lana had forced herself to remain on the throne, clenching the arms so hard she worried the metal might twist under her fingers. As soon as she saw his red robes, muddied at the bottom, more questions sprang to her mind. Then she remembered banishing him just hours earlier.

"Your Highness," he bowed on approach. "How may I be of assistance?"

Lana immediately realised that the adviser was merely paying lip service to her. There was no question or intent behind his words. She tightened her lips and stood up.

"The human requires attention. He has fallen ill."

Tolant glanced towards the chamber but his face remained neutral. Lana waited.

After a while, Tolant shrugged. "I cannot see what this has to do with me, your Highness. As you said, you know your own mind."

Lana let out an exasperated sigh. For once, she would have welcomed his opinion.

"At least go and see him. Find out what happened!"

"As your Highness wishes," Tolant bobbed his head briefly then wheeled around on his heel. Watching him cross the High Hall, Lana returned to her throne. She studied the beams overhead, trying to quell her rising panic. Picking at her nails similarly failed to calm her rushing heartbeat.

Eventually, Tolant ambled out with his hands in his robe pockets. His brows were furrowed. "What's happening?" Lana cried out, her voice betraying her.

The advisor's face twisted. Then he said, almost casually, "It must have been something he ate, your Highness. Perhaps it has disagreed with him."

Lana's eyes darkened. "What did that Captain prepare?"

"I really couldn't say, your Highness. As you know, I was not present when it was brought in." Shrugging again, his shoulders almost reached his ears and he gazed down at the floor with his lips turned down. Then, he looked at her with piercing eyes. "It appears that whatever has caused such illness has yet to finish the human entirely. A quick death might be a kindness."

"No!" Lana flew up, darting into the antechamber. Not noticing Tolant sliding away, her gaze was immediately filled with with human suffering. Curled on the floor, Sigurd's once-ruddy face was white, and he was shivering. His eyes were glossed over, staring ahead at the boots of the young soldier. As she arrived, Sigurd's deep voice let out a rasp. His hand shot out, grasping for something and his head tilted towards the ceiling. "Rognval..." he cried again.

The guard met her shocked eyes. She could tell he was equally at a loss as to what was happening. Lana bent over Sigurd and shook him. He gazed vacantly up at her. He shrugged her arm off then stared back at the floor, muttering to himself. Tears welled up and she blinked to keep them at bay. She tried to control her breathing. His scent was peculiar, whilst there was still a hint of the vitality she had come to know, the edge of it was tinged with darkness. Wrinkling her nose, Lana wasn't sure if the acidic tinge to the air was from him or his effluence. She remembered the sour taste of the ribbons she tasted when they were walking - the taste of sadness, missing those in Valhalla.

Lana cast around the wood panelled chamber. Searching for something, anything, which would ground her rising panic. Only the two guards were there, they couldn't be expected to know what to do either. The room was empty but for a chair and the platters. No human comforts of any sort to help ease his pain.

But, there was someone who knew human-kind. Lana

turned again to Sigurd, "Hold on," she begged. "Please, just...don't die! Don't go to Valhalla yet! I need you." Brushing a rogue tear away with her sleeve, she flew out.

CHAPTER 18 - WALL WRECKING

"Issam!" Lana shouted. Her wings carried her swiftly out of the Hall of horrors. "I need Issam the spy!"

Her call echoed down corridors, sending the lurking worker fae scurrying away from the atrium. She flew towards her chambers, but Issam stepped out into the corridor to meet her. Terrified, but brave.

"Issam!" Lana's voice broke, and the fae realised he had mistaken anger for anguish. "You must tell me."

She drew him into a nearby doorway and set down. Keeping a firm grasp on his arm, she blurted, "The human we took - he ate something which has made him ill."

Issam swallowed then nodded, "Did he eject the food?"

"Yes, I think so," Lana said, "but he is still unwell! Shaking and pale."

Issam drew a blank. "Does Lord Tolant not know what to do?"

Lana sighed, "He..." She shook her head. "He suggested that Sigurd ingested something which disagreed. That was his opinion. As to a cure, no. He made no suggestions. It doesn't matter what Tolant thinks. Sigurd must live. I will not accept that it is kinder to end his suffering."

Frustration and fear were rising in her once more. She paused and breathed in to calm herself. Scaring the spy served no purpose, and she needed answers.

"You have watched the humans, what is this malady? What can stop it?"

Thinking still, Issam cautioned, "The humans have many illnesses, your Highness. Sometimes they eject the food from their mouths when they have eaten too much - or had an excess of the amber liquid which warms them. Could it be that? Seawater perhaps, riding on boats can make them eject also?"

"No." She dismissed the thought that Sigurd was poorly because of something they had done earlier in the day. He hadn't ingested saltwater, and she thought he was unlikely to sail as much had he implied they did if it made him poorly.

"He is lying on the floor and clenching his torso. He didn't know me, or who I was. Shouting out also, calling for something, but I don't know what. It's..."

She tried to find the right words to make him understand, "It's as if he can see something which isn't there?" Despite her own experiences with the intangible yet definitely present Lifeforce, she wasn't entirely sure the spy could relate.

"Do you think he has travelled to another place? In his mind, I mean?" Issam still sounded confused.

"I don't know, and I don't think we could get him to explain either. His words are not like ours at all. You wouldn't understand."

Issam pulled back, a little affronted. "Your Highness," he said, "I have witnessed many strange things about these new humans. Rituals where they seem to lose all sense of where they are. Sometimes they ingest some dried herbs, a kind of fungus maybe, which they brought with them. Other times their chanting alone causes it. They are not as simple as our humans are."

Lana looked curious, "Do you think that concoction is what he ate then? How did he get it? He was singing before it happened."

"No," Issam answered firmly. "Not if this effect is so sudden and he is still so unwell. Their rituals take many hours, much preparation."

"Then you think Tolant is right?"

Issam pushed his lips together and frowned. Reaching for a vague memory, he held up a finger. Lana breathed out a long breath as she waited for him to answer.

"If it is something he ate, it's usually a plant that's to blame. Animals don't seem to cause the same problem. The humans - our islanders, that is - have remedies."

"For this illness?"

"If it is a poison, then they try to treat it, yes. They take the blackened wood from a furious fire, then crush it with the white rocks which crumble. Then they give it to the human. It usually works."

Lana felt a flicker of hope enter her heart. "Where do we get these things from?"

Quick to answer, Issam offered, "I can fetch charcoal from the fae metalwork camps, but the white rocks are much further away."

"Where?"

Issam shook his head, "It would take me many hours to reach Westray, your Highness. When I have seen the villagers prepare this paste, the wise woman has the right things to hand and give it to the sick person as soon as possible."

He looked sad for a moment, lost in the memory of when a small child had been lost after eating the attractive flowers of dead mans' bells from his fingertips. The grey medicine hadn't been given quickly enough and the whole village had mourned. The next day the whole village pulled up the deadly foxglove from their nearby woodland.

Lana shook his arm again, not caring that her grip was hurting. "Where on Westray? Tell me what I'm looking for!"

Issam's eyes flared, "The white rock, your Highness. It runs in seams through the flat stones. The nearest place would be Skel Wick." He knew that the Queen could fly at easily double his speed, maybe faster, should she choose.

Lana flapped her huge wings and she finally dropped Issam's arm. "Fetch the charcoal and whatever else we need to make it. I will return."

*****

On any other day, Lana could have enjoyed flying so low to the green sea beneath her. The sun had started to set. Red and pink clouds above her formed a canopy which added an uneasy glow to her tense flight. As her wings laboured to push her quickly through the cooling air, she considered soaring above them, just to escape their ominous presence. Red. She hated red.

The waves beneath her rose and fell. As soon as she saw them begin to form crests, she looked ahead, searching the grey coastline for a white streak. The flat landscape rising past the beaches was familiar to her, but she had paid it scant attention before now. This time, she flew closer. The risk of being seen was immense, but desperation drove her to endanger herself.

The sea underneath her was dark, seaweed clung to stone shelves dying the shallow water a deep green. Lana scanned ahead as she skirted the edges of the rocky shoreline. Folding sandstones exposed deep crevices, but she had yet to spot the line of white she needed. Occasional sandy beaches brightened the jagged grey, framed by ridges of wave-dulled stoney teeth running into the water.

Her wings were tiring, breathing laboured. Lana set down on one such stretch of sand and paused to look around. Inland a little, she could see wisps of smoke rising. The smell of roasting pricked at her nostrils, and she turned away from the low wind pushing this unpalatable scent towards her. The last glimmers of sunlight urged her to be quick.

She walked up the beach, to where a low rise of rocks lay. Closer examination of the flat stones proved futile. Even underneath the algae, they were definitively grey, through and through. Flying again, she skirted over a small headland and landed the other side of the promontory. More grey slabs.

Lana tried to quell a rising sense of despondency. Cursing herself for never having spent the time getting to know the landscape. If she had only flown lower when travelling to the ceremonies, she might have seen where this white rock was!

Another bay, equally unproductive. The light was almost gone. She kicked out at the layers of sandstone. Gritting her teeth, partly from the pain in her foot, she flew around to the next inlet. From the corner of her eye, she glimpsed a flash of something inland. Wheeling around to look closer, hawk like vision narrowed in on something grayish-white. Nearly obscured by moss, a mass of stones piled into a low wall. Some parts had recently crumbled away, revealing a chalky interior.

She flew over, her heart thumping with expectancy. On the ground, smaller slabs of the rock had toppled from the wall and smashed, revealing seams of light grey. She scratched one with her fingernail, leaving a groove of pure white. Lana smiled before realising that the seam was very thin. It would take her hours to scrape off sufficient quantities. Not that the spy had been specific, but she thought more than a scratching would be required. And, she hadn't thought to bring a bowl or sack to collect it in.

Lana chewed her lip as she picked the chalk from underneath her fingernail. Studying the stones in the half light of dusk, there was no other option. She had to find one with a richer seam.

Systematically, she began to dismantle the wall. Wrenching the tightly packed boulders apart, she raised and smashed. The first few landed with a dull thud. One bounced the wrong way against another, hurtling onto her ankle. The shock jolted her, and she re-focused on more careful selection and aim. Taking out her frustration, she found a rhythm of grabbing and hurling, exhaling as she heaved the stones ever harder. As the rock pile grew, the thudding turned into a more satisfying clunk. Stones smashing stones.

She had reduced the height of the already low stretch of wall by some thirty or so slabs before one finally broke apart on impact. Lana picked up the pieces, heavy in her hands. The head-sized piece of rock had cleft entirely in two, both sides exposed the creamy whiteness she sought. She dug her fingernail in and scraped. Again and again she gouged until she reached the sandstone. Her fingertip was halfway sunken into the dip when she stopped.

She sighed with relief, surely such an expanse of limestone would yield enough for the cure? She picked up both halves of the stone and took off. The extra weight felt insignificant as she flew home with hope in her heart.

CHAPTER 19 – RECOVERY

Cool hands lifted his head up. Sigurd drowsily let his lips fall apart, the accompanying agony of moving swept over him and his stomach clenched once more. A foul tasting paste was shoved into his mouth, claggy on his tongue. Then, firm fingers held his chin to his upper jaw. His tongue twisted inside his mouth trying to rid itself of the gritty coating. He tried to jerk his head away, and his eyes flew open.

Not able to focus, the smell of fir tugged him back to a vague understanding of where he was. "Eat," a female voice commanded. Somehow he trusted it.

His mouth filled with saliva as he masticated the paste. His mind reached to identify the taste, but all he could think of was the time when Rognval had won a winter's fight and pushed him into a dying fire. The cauldron hanging over had tipped remnants of broth over him as it clunked the back of his head.

This was not that time though. No laughter accompanied the pains that shot through him still. The image of Rognval, victoriously raising his fist to cheers of appreciation, faded. Sigurd swallowed. The burning began to fade.

*****

Sigurd groaned, more from the bright light which had appeared overhead than because he was trying to say something. He brought a heavy arm up to shield his eyes. The halos around blurry head shapes diminished as his vision adjusted. With his other hand, he felt the warm wooden floor he was lying on. Then he reached to feel for his sword. Patting about his midriff, Sigurd realised that there was nothing covering him but an under-tunic. He checked his neck. His hammer was missing!

Feeling more naked from the lack of weapon than his scant attire, Sigurd tried to sit up. His joints felt painful, arms wobbly. Eventually, he heaved his upper body off the floor and sat with his legs stretched in front of him. He waited for his head to stop spinning the room.

Performing a quick visual check of himself, because he didn't trust his own senses, there appeared nothing amiss or missing. The heaviness in his limbs suggested he had been beaten to close to death, but he was rather surprised to see unblemished flesh.

He looked around the unfamiliar area. Watching over him, two soldiers. His recovery prompted one to silently turn and leave. Sigurd stretched a little, turning his head to identify his surroundings. At least it definitely wasn't the earthen cell. The wooden panels were familiar in style, but different to the chamber he had last been in. Eaten in. Before the nausea overtook him. He remembered.

Bile rose in his throat and Sigurd looked around for a receptacle. Finding none, he swallowed it back down, realising that the reaction was more reflex than urge. His mouth still felt gritty though. What had they given him?

"Water?" Sigurd asked, miming to drink. The guard passed him a cup of brackish liquid. Draining it, he asked for more. As he sipped the refill a little slower, Sigurd studied the fae in front of him.

Was this the same one who had been present when he was ill? Sigurd thought it might have been, and felt compelled to express his gratitude. When his torturer had visited, standing over him with a sneering smile watching his pain, this bold guard had prevented him from approaching closer. Sigurd vaguely remembered a look of surprise on the robed man's face when a sword had appeared across his mid-section. Sigurd rubbed his half ear, as if to remind himself of his innate ability to survive, even against the greatest of odds.

His hand flew to his neck - the torturer had done something! Before the guard stopped him, the fae had pulled off his hammer! Sigurd groaned. It might have been just a neck piece to some, but the absence of it threatened Sigurd. Uneasiness washed over him. Although he wasn't as superstitious as many, that hammer had been with him through battles and death, and he wanted it back. And, now that he thought of it, he wanted those figures from the settlement back. The torturer had taken them too, and seemed pleased about it. These items connected him to his roots when at times he felt only the faintest of tethers otherwise. He wondered why the fae had taken them?

He tapped his chest, "Sigurd." Looking the guard, his eyes asked the question which few did.

"Uffer," the fae answered. His voice didn't have the depth

of Sigurd's.

"Thank you for your help before," Sigurd said. Of course, the soldier had no idea what he was saying, but a brief lift of his lips showed he understood Sigurd's intention.

"Skol!" Sigurd lifted the cup at the guard, then drank again.

The door flew open and Lana rushed in. She pulled herself up short just before she reached him. A wary look crossed her face. Sigurd grinned, remembering the smell of fir trees. He could almost feel her studying the wrinkles of his skin. He held out his hand.

She hesitated briefly, then shyly moved closer to take his fingers in her own. A tentative smile began to stretch over that oval face he had grown to care for. His heart swelled and he clutched her fingers tightly. The feeling of relief grew and his eyes moistened.

He blinked away the emotion, before realising that her dark eyes were also brimming.

"You can leave us now," she ordered, twisting her head towards the guard, her voice wavery.

Lana waited until the door had closed before looking at him again. The familiar fizzle between them ignited.

"You gave me medicine," Sigurd stated.

She nodded.

"It worked." He screwed his face up in an exaggerated grimace, then chewed with an empty mouth.

Lana laughed softly. "I wasn't sure it would. Someone told me of a human remedy which we tried."

Sigurd stroked his thumb over her soft hand. "I have

thanks you tried."

"Sigurd..." Lana hesitated, her eyes welling up again. "Sigurd, I was afraid. I had not known what fear really was until I met you."

He dropped her hand and moved closer to trace his fingers along her jaw as she dipped her head.

"Then I feared I had lost you. Done something to make you ill."

"Not have fear," he said tenderly. "I am here. I will not go."

"But you must," she wailed. "You must tell the others not to come. But I couldn't bear it if you went."

"Do you want me to go?"

Lana shook her head. He slid his hand down her arm, taking her hand in his. "Then I won't."

He felt a tear fall on his wrist. Drawing her into his muscular arms, he cradled her as she released the anguish. He stroked soft long hair, and clutched her tightly to his chest when the sobs intensified. Sigurd found himself crooning - the same lullaby his mother had used when he was young and needed comfort.

Gradually the crying eased. She pulled back, momentarily ashamed of her outburst. Sigurd tipped her head towards his, and gently thumbed away the wet streaks. Her dark eyes wavered with uncertainty, but Sigurd had never been so sure of the intimacy he now sought. He leaned in and joined his lips with hers.

The frisson of energy between them darted through to his core. Sensing her tentative response to his kiss, he felt their passion rise. Deeper and deeper he sank into her mouth, inhaling the heady scent of her. In return, she slid her arms tightly around him, pulling him closer.

Hands roamed over clothes, touching, caressing. The need to feel her bare skin against his overtook all caution, and he pulled apart from her to tear off his tunic. Her eyes darkened, not with anger, but awe as she drank in his naked chest. Slim fingers traced a scar, gathered many years ago and now just a puckered line, which ran from shoulder to his ribs. He knew his size was intimidating to some women, and the fae were slight of build. But he wasn't worried. Sigurd knew his strength attracted her, and he knew his gentleness had been much praised before.

Sigurd let her absorb his broad chest for a moment before his need to touch her again grew too much. Drawing his hands up her arms, he slipped his fingers through the loops holding her jade dress on her shoulders. Dropping one narrow band down, he paused. Trying to check if this was an approved action, but failing to find the right words.

Lana stiffened. Behind, her enormous green wings rose into his view. So close, the translucent panes mesmerised him. Diverted completely from his earlier, earthier desire, Sigurd reached out to touch them. She pulled back, uncertainty spreading across her face.

Sigurd chuckled and lowered his arm. Her eyebrows gathered.

"It alright," Sigurd said, his eyes cast around the room. "Perhaps here not a comfortable place!" His blue eyes twinkled at her again. "But I want some day to..." He reached out a finger and caressed the bare skin on her arm whilst looking at her wings.

"It's not that," she glanced over her shoulder towards the door. Then, her head bowed and she studied her gown, correcting herself. "It *is* that. But I don't know your ways of touching."

Sigurd's mouth dropped. Of course, why would she? He realised also that he had no idea what to truly expect underneath her figure hugging robes. Were the fae built the same way as humans? Looking down at his hands, still tingling with the afterglow of her touch, he felt a little stupid. His arrogance in assuming that the intimacy he sought would be compatible with her!

"I am sorry." He shook his head.

"No!" Lana said, and took his hand once more. "You teach me, and I will teach you more of our language, our words."

Sigurd breathed in deeply, and exhaled very slowly. The throbbing in his groin abated slightly, although he suspected with this magnificent creature in his presence and mind, it would never go away entirely.

"I like your touch," Lana said wistfully. Through his eyelashes, he could see her wrestling with something. His heart flopped over.

"Oh *gudine*," he sighed, "and I like your touch. Too much!"

One side of his mouth pulled up and he drew her back into his arms. She nestled into his chest. Sigurd felt her ribs expand as she breathed him deeply in. He dropped a small

147

kiss on top of her head, feeling a slight tug in his mind. It was as if something which was tangled up there relaxed. Tiredness washed over him.

"I need sleep," he mumbled.

Lana sat up and smiled. Her eyes seemed oddly glassy, not with tears, but hazy somehow. In a smooth movement, she unfurled herself from him and stood. "I will find you a more comfortable place to rest." Sigurd suddenly felt so sleepy, it was all he could do to nod. As soon as she had gone, he laid back down on the floor and closed his eyes.

CHAPTER 20 - REFLECTION

A few days after Sigurd began his recovery, the Captain approached Lana and Sigurd returning from an early morning walk in the forest. With no knowledge of the subterfuge by which it had been called, he announced that the Council was assembled and awaited her attendance.

Lana's good mood was instantly dulled. "I do not recall that there was a meeting due?" She said, more to herself than to question the Captain.

Lana frowned, annoyed by his announcement and with herself. Distracted by Sigurd, she had lost track of the days a little. They had fallen into a pleasant routine since his illness - exploring Naturae, chatting, playing their mime game. She greatly enjoyed his company, especially when he held her. Contrary to Tolant's advice, she felt quite safe with him. Once the day was over, and he was resting or eating in his new room on the other side of the palace, she visited the Pupaetory and tried to feed the vines. Part of her had become convinced that if she spent enough time with him, absorbed in his energy, his Lifeforce would eventually build up sufficiently for more than a few wisps of happiness to trickle out of her and into the starving cocoons.

Alone at night, though, the guilt at neglecting the rest of her duties gnawed away. Somehow, being with him seemed justified at the time. When they were together, she thought of nothing else but him. He was teaching her so much about his customs, his homeland, and learning her language so quickly. She was sure that it was all useful information.

She asked the guards, who had followed the Captain on his quest to find her, to escort Sigurd to his chambers. As they left, accompanied by the - now explained - action of blowing kisses at each other, she began to worry. She didn't think Sigurd especially needed guarding - although his strength was returning - but she maintained the public illusion that he was kept under close watch. With any luck, the Council wouldn't see him being returned to the bedroom which she had designated for him to rest in. Naturae was usually quiet when there was no court in session. And yet, because of her absence, she had completely failed to notice the arrival of the Council members.

As she flew out of the room and down the passages, Lana mentally counted the days which had passed. The thought then occurred to her that she wasn't incorrect in her earlier confusion over dates. Officially, the Council convened on alternate months, to allow Nobles to spend sufficient time in their lands and travel back and forth to Naturae. Court gathered prior to and after a ceremony, and not otherwise. Sometimes the Council meeting coincided, at other times of the year, not. She hadn't forgotten a planned assembly at all.

Another idea entered her head as she flew down the corridors, one which caused her hand to shake as she fumbled with the door. Was this how it had begun for her mother? Unannounced meetings? Had her mother known what she was walking into before she had been murdered?

Thinking back, she tried to dredge the memories of the

hours before that encounter from the depths of her mind. Panicking now, she found a void where the memory should be. Buried away, not spoken of, the horror of her murder had long since been pushed into a box.

She shut the door behind her and abandoned trying to remember the past. With eyes which had filled with unwanted tears, she began to pace the room. It was only a matter of time before someone came and knocked with a repeated request for her presence. She forced herself to focus on something more pleasant to counteract the mounting dread.

Sigurd instantly sprang into her head. His smile. The creases around his eyes. His gentle touch. Holding hands with him, that feeling of security he gave her. As if no-one else mattered but her. The intensity of his gaze when he looked at her.

She swallowed back down the fear and continued her automatic pacing.

It was only when she had checked off the mental list of things in their right places did she start to consider the changes he had wrought since his arrival. Not only had the thought of him calmed her, but even as she scrutinized the neat room, there was something different about her routine. All was as it should be. She realised that she wasn't as bothered though, as she would have been were it not absolute perfection. The bed was made, the window clear, the floor swept.

Her usual compulsion to arrange things was absent - partly because she was spending less time here, nothing was out of place. Except herself, she understood, looking in the mirror.

Her hair hung loosely around her shoulders, tangled from the winds and walking. Although her crown still held it down, the silver hadn't been polished for a while and the lustre had faded. Her gown was rumpled, slightly askew from the gentle caresses they had shared earlier. Lana smiled as she remembered the encounter. She peeled off the dress, regardless.

She reluctantly shrugged off that Lana and attired herself as a Queen. Funny, she had once thought a Queen was all that she was, but now she wasn't so sure.

After brushing her hair and replacing the silver circle, she stared once again in the mirror. Her heart sank a little. The regal figure reflected there no longer looked familiar, or quite how she now felt inside. But, it was who the Council were expecting.

She raised her chin as she studied her reflection. She was not her mother. She would not allow them the satisfaction of a surprise assault the former Queen had perhaps endured. She was different. She was loved. And yet, she was also Lana. Lana held her head high and looked down her nose at her image. A Queen to be feared!

CHAPTER 21 - INTERVENTION

Rounding the corner and flying in through the doors of the High Hall, by the time Lana reached her throne, defiance had shifted to anger. Hovering above the dais, she spun around and glared at the rows of faces seated before her.

"On whose authority do you attend today?" The demand caused confusion amongst the Nobles and ambassadors present. Some turned and whispered to each other, nervously flicking glances at their Queen.

"Well? Is nobody going to answer a direct question?"

One of the European ambassadors spoke up, "We understood the command to convene was on your orders, your Highness?"

The small group all nodded, looking at each other and back to her as if this was ordinary.

"Since when do we assemble outside of the scheduled times? Did you not question it?" Lana's voice started to sound shrill, even to her.

The Nobles (the few who had actually turned up at least) looked down, whereas the six ambassadors began to rummage around in their deep pockets. They had flown a large distance, across many lands and expected a warmer welcome for their hasty efforts. One produced a small scroll and stood, then bowed as he proffered it to her.

Lana flew down and plucked it from his fingers. As she read, her eyes grew wide.

"Who else had a note such as this?" She demanded.

More tiny kestrel scrolls were passed forwards. Each was in a slightly different faelore script to the next, but all contained roughly the same message.

Royal Council member:

Queen commands your return immediately to appoint a guardian. Naturae is at risk.

"Tolant!" She wheeled around, looking for the adviser. He was usually to be found lurking in the corners behind the dais, but not today.

"Tolant!" Lana screeched. She had not seen him at all lately, come to think of it. Not since Sigurd had been ill. Despite sending him away just prior to that, the adviser had clearly still been skulking around. Even if he hadn't proved helpful during Sigurd's illness, the palace was functioning as normal. Wisely then, he had kept himself and his opinions scarce.

"Where is he?" She hissed at the guards on either side of her throne. They looked at each other then faced their Queen with blank faces.

"Fetch him!"

Lana turned back to the Council, gritting her teeth so hard her lips almost disappeared into the tightness of her face. The ancient fae before her shuffled in their seats, waiting to see what she would do next. Protocol dictated that the Queen would welcome them and open the meeting by deciding who should speak and when. It was less of a discussion, more of a demand and answer. Lana rarely asked for advice, although some subtly sought to offer it.

The silence quickly grew oppressive. Lana sat on her throne and waited for Tolant to arrive. Out of habit, she arranged her skirts so they fell smoothly. Much as though she tried to quell the rising panic inside her, counterbalancing it was anger. Fury at being forced into such a position. Were they here to do the same to her as they had done to her mother? She studied their persons in turn, checking their robes for the obvious signs of weaponry. But then, a dagger is a small blade...

"Your Highness?" Young Ambassador Spenser, from one of the European states, hesitantly spoke up. Lana flicked her eyes over him. "We..." and he cast his arm around to include the congregation. "Can only imagine your surprise at our appearance. We also are surprised to see you."

The fae all nodded. Some murmured platitudes.

"We, and I believe I speak for us all, are very relieved to find you safe and well, indeed." The Ambassador bowed, feeling he had the support of his peers behind him.

Lana sat up taller, "I am quite sure you are." She looked again at the note. "If I were to receive such a missive, however, I would question who had sent it."

"So," Spenser continued, "the Queendom is well? Thriving as usual?"

Lana remembered now with a jolt. She hardened her face, refusing to let the fear show on it. This ambassador's family had been one of those who had slit her mother's throat. The Spensers. Not this particular fae of course - but a brother or something. She trusted none of them anyway.

"There is nothing remiss at all." Lana's calm lie didn't quite have the impact she hoped for. The Nobles from territories in England flushed. Rumours from the last court session were doubtless rife about the absence of some of their number.

"As you can see, everything is as it should be. No change necessary."

One of the Nobles coughed, and she glared at him. "Unless one of you has something to say?" Lana asked icily. The elder fae resumed their study of the floor.

Ambassador Spenser glanced over them and sniffed. "Quite," he deferred. "Are we therefore to assume that there is no urgency to appoint a new overseer of Naturae after all?"

Lana scowled. "There is no need at all. Everything is in hand."

"It is just..." The Ambassador tailed off as the doors behind the gathered fae flew open. Tolant skulked in, flanked by her two guards. Lana's eyes narrowed.

"Lord Tolant, how good of you to finally join us." Her mouth tightened as she took in her errant advisor's usual threadbare robes of office. "Perhaps you could enlighten us as to why you felt it necessary to call a meeting of the Council - in my name - without consulting me?"

Lana expected the adviser to look shifty, but strangely he

seemed to straighten as he approached the group. "Your Highness forgets," he said innocently, "I hoped you would remember our discussion?"

Ignoring her raised eyebrows and accompanying glare, Tolant cast his beady eyes over the Council. "Perhaps, with all of the confusion over the human..." Lana just knew he was smirking as he turned away from her. Her wings rose behind her.

But, rather than bawl him out as she would normally have done, her voice was controlled and frosty. "I have not forgotten anything. Including my banishment of you, Lord Tolant."

The council members drew in their breaths collectively.

"Did you think that I wouldn't know? Did you assume that I was too weak minded to figure out whose underhand tactics were responsible for this meeting?"

Tolant turned to see his Queen looming over him. The pieces fell into place as Lana spoke. "Did you expect me to stand for this?" Her face was practically touching his. She could smell the betrayal and fear rising from him.

Tolant's eyes darted to Ambassador Spenser's, almost pleading for his intervention.

"Guards!"

The shout had been anticipated by the experienced soldiers, who had seen her rise in anger many times before. They were by Tolant's side within the flap of a wing.

"Your Highness! The Council...?" Tolant attempted to inject an indulgent tone into his voice, whilst all the while, his desperate eyes cast around for support.

Lana gritted her teeth, "Restrain him and put him in the Beneath," she hissed.

CHAPTER 22 – BRAVE FACE

The council members watched Tolant's extraction with mixed emotions. Ever-present in such meetings usually, he had been a useful ally to them. Through his formerly close relationship with the Queen, the ageing adviser, who they believed had faithfully served for all of his life, provided a back route to her ears. However, it looked like this avenue of influence was firmly closed now.

Wary faces turned to face the Queen once more in silence. Although slightly proud of herself for reining in her temper, Lana was in a quandary. The betrayal of her most trusted adviser more than rankled, even though their relationship had been distinctly more fractious since Sigurd's arrival. Now she realised that her position was, as her mothers had been, still precarious.

Taking a moment to gather her thoughts, Lana landed and walked slowly to her throne. Her back was turned to the assembled fae so that none would see the conflicting emotions flashing over her face. Wings still flapping, ready if necessary. She felt braver with such an action as well. If they did plan to stab her or make a move towards her person, she would hear them. If nothing else, her superior wing size and speed meant she would prove a difficult target to hit.

Right now, she thought they were as shocked as she at the

turn of events. But next time, who knew what they would plan? She could never let her guard down again - that much was apparent. She refused to make the same mistakes as her mother, nor allow the Council to influence her judgment. Let them think they had a say in how she ran her Queendom? No. She had long suspected that other voices muddied decision making. Indeed, she had held off deciding as the clamour of land-grabbing was too confusing. She told herself that was why, at least.

Although they had no powers like hers, Nobles were elder fae, originally the ancients. Closely connected, and sharing common roots, their origins long ago forgotten. The Council, representing both the lands which fell under her dominion, as well as the other fae communities across the regions of Europe and beyond, had been established as a mechanism to share knowledge. Information which was universal to all fae, but relevant to her Queendom. They were advisory in capacity. Only she had the ability to create, and bless. Therefore, only she had the truest power. As Lana sat and faced the Council, her mind resolved. She would pay no more than lip service to their advice.

The first hint that this would be a harder strategy to maintain came when Ambassador Spenser once again stood up. Then the Lord of Mercia rose to his feet, folding his hands and waited patiently for her attention. One of the Ambassadors from the reaches of northern Europe pulled himself into a hunched stand, somewhat slowly as he was tired. Lana flicked her eyes over them. Although Spenser glowed with vitality, the other two looked ailing.

"You appear to be in need of sustenance," Lana said, not mocking nor enquiring, merely observing.

Lord Duanei glanced up at her. In his ancient dark eyes, she saw sorrow, as well as exhaustion.

"My Queen," he began, in a grave, weary voice. "Since we are gathered here, I feel compelled to inform you again. In Mercia, and other parts of the country of England, we are encountering difficulties with the settlements. As you know, since the Sation wars, the attendance at the ceremonies has been dwindling. With the spread of other forms of worship - these 'churches'- your Highness, we are struggling to keep the people's attention. To persuade them to return to our ways."

Lana nodded, this was not a recent problem. The Sation wars had essentially been a result of the rising popularity of the new Christian faith sweeping through the world. The vampires had won the race to influence its direction, and they were proving extremely resourceful in persuading the mortals to convert. Churches, which had been initially viewed as a possible medium for alternative worship of the fae, were now places where the vampires built trust amongst the humans. Living and feeding within their ranks in ever more plain sight. A feat not practical for the winged fae.

"I will still attend your planned ceremonies, Lord Duanei." Lana intended to reassure the old Noble. "Your responsibility remains to ensure the people gather. Do what you must to get them there."

"That's just the problem, your Highness."

Lana's eyes narrowed. "Why would it be an issue? There

are surely still believers? Ones who have benefited from my blessings in the past and will want to do so again? Or have they all defected to the churches?" Just what she needed now - a vampire conflict.

Lord Duanei stared nervously at her. "The settlements on the coasts have been targeted by other humans. Raging ones, with no respect for our ways." He added, "Or Christian ways."

Lana's eyes flashed around the room - the other Nobles looked equally shifty. "Has this happened in your areas as well?" Some shook their heads but were clearly afraid. One or two nodded, guilty fear also flashing across their faces.

"They land in long boats. Hordes of them ravage what they can, and then leave again. I believe some of the villages are talking about trying to arrange some kind of accord with them, but they are living under their threat constantly. Negotiation is impossible. Slaughter seems to be all that they know."

"I should have been told of this earlier." Lana looked up to the ceiling for fear her face would betray her. Deflecting seemed the only way to navigate what she already knew was a dire issue facing the islands closest to Naturae.

"Your Highness, we tried. We informed Lord Tolant of it as soon as we heard what was happening!"

Lana gritted her teeth.

Lord Duanei, sensing he had her complete attention now, became bolder. "It is a very serious matter, and I am surprised it took as long as this for you to call us here to discuss it."

"I did not assemble you!" Lana flew instantly into a

temper. "I knew nothing of this." Her fury at Tolant grew. How could he have kept this knowledge for so long? This was confirmation that the invaders were not just affecting her locality. "I did not receive your reports."

"And what of the dominions in Europe?" Lana demanded, glaring at the ambassadors. Shifting the Nobles' focus to elsewhere had worked before when tricky questions were raised.

With typical nonchalance, the representatives present shook their heads. Ambassador Spenser spoke up.

"With the greatest of respect, your Highness, we are a far larger and more spread out populous. These raiders have yet to impact us."

Lana sighed in exasperation. The Fae in Europe had always considered themselves more protected. They had also suffered during the Sation wars and, in fact, the prevalence of the new Christian religion was rumoured to be greater there than it was in her Queendom.

Spenser, who seemed to have decided he spoke for all six of the ambassadorial delegation, pointed out glibly, "This seems to be a localised issue. Although, if you cannot reverse the situation, then I am sure that our Councils in Europe would have to look at intervention."

There it was again - the threat. Lana's face froze, she absolutely did not want them to try and force her removal. There was no line of succession yet, true, but her mother and her mother's mother had held this Queendom for thousands of years. Unfortunately Lana had not even contrived her own back-up plan. Details on how to pupate a Royal were vague at best and Lana never had a chance to cross-examine her mother on the subject.

But the Ambassador hadn't finished. "Lord Tolant mentioned something about a human?"

Lana's mouth tightened. Her heart thumped.

"And some confusion? I believe the Revenants Treaty states that we fae are not permitted to directly interact with humans?" He raised an eyebrow at her.

Lana breathed out slowly through her nose. Weighing up in her mind what he could know. For sure, he would not be talking to Tolant ever again, but had he seen anything else? Heard other whispers perhaps?

"I only ask..." Ambassador Spenser continued, "because I have a duty to report to my own Queen if there are any indications that the Treaty, which took her over five decades to negotiate with the Vampire Assembly, is at risk."

He started to walk in front of the dais, gathering steam for his next threat. "I would hate to dishonour your family line any further. Your own reign having proved so stable over the last two hundred years..."

He turned to meet her eyes, with a young face so full of purpose and intent Lana felt cool inside.

Lana's mind whirled. Usually, in such a situation, she relied upon Tolant to smooth ruffled feathers with a glib placation. Lying was not something which she was very good at. Directly avoiding the truth was equally not her forte. Neither was appeasement. Or diplomacy.

"Ambassador, I assure you that there is nothing untoward about what Lord Tolant said. We have not been engaging with the humans at all - except as permitted by the Treaty." She tried her hardest to meet his eyes with an unyielding glower.

"Even these recent ones?" The Ambassador gazed over the Noble Council members, who all shook their heads vehemently.

"You see," Lana said sweetly, attempting to mollify the fae. "As I said, there is nothing to concern you at all."

"Except the invaders," Lord Duanei butted in.

"Which I will consider how we can manage..." Lana continued to soothe. She could not begin to try and work out which was the bigger threat to her right now. Both Sigurd's countrymen and the threat of European intervention had devastating consequences.

Ambassador Spenser dipped his head, just for a moment. He then sat back down again.

Lana drew herself up to her full height and grasped what remained of her command. "I will see to it that you are provided with some live Lifeforce before you all depart." As if she was a gracious host, Lana bowed her head at the council before flying over their heads and out. No-one noticed the tremor in her hands.

CHAPTER 23 – THE PROMISE

Lana slammed the door to Sigurd's quarters behind her. She assumed the guards would disperse as ordered from the hallway. Nothing gave away the presence of something untoward like a pair of soldiers outside.

Sigurd sat up in the low bed, pulled out of his post meal nap by the noise.

"My Queen," he said, rising and approaching her. "What is the matter?"

Lana's eyes were filled with tears, and she kept pacing around the room. Her hands were shaking and her wings beat in time with her steps. Sigurd touched her arm, gently pulling her to a stop. She gazed up at him, and his heart wrenched. Thin red lips wobbled. Sigurd pulled her into his arms and laid his head on top of hers. He had never seen her in such distress, but instinctively knew she needed him to settle herself down. He thought it was his warmth or just his touch, but he anticipated a tug of something to leave him as he held her close.

Lana inhaled, feeling the freely given ribbon twirl into her. She allowed it to infuse her, calm her. Sigurd's embrace was a place of sanctuary. Somehow, her burdens were almost unthinkable when his presence surrounded her, blocking out the world.

She pulled back and gazed at him. As they searched each other's eyes, her heart sank with the dread of what she knew she had to request of him, of the pain it meant for her as well. She broke the connection, unable to cope with the intense mix of emotions coursing through her. Buried her head back in his chest. The tears finally fell.

After a few minutes of her sobbing, Sigurd's curiosity won out. "Lana, tell me. Maybe I can help?"

This seemingly simple offer brought on renewed sobs. Lana buried her head in his arms. It seemed to her that the last person who could offer her assistance was the only one genuinely wanting to try. The only being willing to support her in this most desperate time of need, was the very cause of the issues.

"Please, at least let me try?"

"You must go," Lana blurted out, no longer able to keep it in.

"I will not leave you, I said that."

"I know," Lana said, looking up at him finally. "But you must go back to your kin on Rousay."

Sigurd looked bewildered. During the last few days, he had almost forgotten about the others he left on the islands they had attacked. Conveniently pushed away the guilt about failing to make good on his deathbed promise to Rognval.

He was also just grateful to be alive. Getting to know Lana, mysterious though she was, he thought she felt the same way as he did. He had even wondered if she might be what he had been unconsciously searching for, all these years. Someone who could accept his eccentricities, be amused by them even. Someone who he could care for. Somebody who needed him as much as he needed them.

He had no doubt that Lana saw his hugr and accepted it. Her patience with him, her dedication to trying to help him understand, touched him deeply. That it cost him something, perhaps his luck - his hamingja - was of lesser consequence. He gave it freely, in return for her acceptance of his peculiar hugr. That she now wished to push him away hurt more than he could find her words for. Just as he realised that he loved her.

"I thought you wanted me to stay?"

"I do!" Lana paused, "But it isn't safe for you. I cannot keep you hidden here. I cannot keep you alive."

He nodded. A part of him knew she had been trying to keep him separate, but his untameable urges to do what he felt like doing at that very moment placed them both in jeopardy. He doubted that even if he was restrained in the Beneath he could resist his own nature.

"And, I cannot kill you," Lana said bleakly.

Sigurd's blinked. The thought of his own death had been far from his mind in recent days, but now he worried again. Sooner or later, the torturer would reappear. Somehow he understood that the creature would find a way to hurt him again. Despite the fact that he still had no answers to his questions, other than knowing the urges of his countryfolk and their need to explore. Inevitably, more like him would find these isles. Without being constantly in Lana's presence, his position here suddenly felt rocky once more. Regardless of her declaration, he abruptly realised he was on borrowed time.

Lana decided not to expand on the reason why he was protected. She looked around the dimly lit room, to avoid meeting his eyes. Autumn approached and the open apertures of the window let in a chilly breeze. There was a ceremony due in a moon-turn, the last before the great harvesting, and her final land blessing of the year was expected.

Perhaps there was a way to solve both problems, she wondered. She stood and turned to face him.

"We - I - need you to return to the villages and the people you came with. You cannot tell the villagers, whomever is left at least, of what you know of Naturae. Who and what we are, where we live - they cannot know. The islanders do not notice us; it is enough that they believe in the 'Gud' who they worship."

Sigurd felt the snap in her change of focus. Inside, he recognised they shared the ability to switch from one emotion to another in the blink of an eye. Shifting her crushing fear to conviction in her voice. He let her carry on, watching as she began to walk around the room again.

"And your kind. Your people," she stared at him with serious eyes. "You must impress upon them that they have to allow the villagers to attend the ceremony at the big stone circle."

She studied his face as he absorbed what she was dictating. Content that he was concentrating, she continued. "I have explained the necessity of this to you already. It is more important than you can possibly understand that the autumn ceremony - the ritual as you call it - occurs."

A nod of his head satisfied Lana that he comprehended what she was saying.

"I can try," he said eventually. "Now I can speak something like their language - your language - I can try." Then he frowned, "But convincing my men to let them go will not be easy."

"You must do more than that. Your people must get the islanders - all the people who remain on the islands you have attacked - to go to the circle. To honour their customs."

Sigurd barked a laugh.

"My Queen, you do not understand what you are asking me to do!"

He shook his dreadlocks away, still chuckling in disbelief.

"Sigurd," Lana knelt down by his knees and laid a hand on the warm leather. "You must. My Queendom depends on it. Everything you see here, depends on it. The circles of Faeth must be attended."

He looked at her. She was serious. Shaking his head he looked away. Out of the window he could faintly see the mists which protected the magic, whose held secrets he had only just begun to uncover.

"I cannot tell the villagers that what they believe is true, and I am to tell my people that what they believe is false?"

"You have no choice," she whispered. "I have no choice."

His eyes swivelled down to her head.

"What if I don't? What if I can't?"

Lana mumbled, "Then you, and I, will be killed. And nothing will ever be the same again."

Again, Sigurd knew she meant it.

The silence hung between them as both contemplated her idea. It seemed there was little other option. Both logical and illogical at the same time.

Eventually, he said in a quiet voice, "I will try, my love. I promise, I will try."

Lana's eyes filled and she squeezed his hand, afraid she would change her mind and keep him with her if she tried to speak.

"Will I ever see you again?" Sigurd asked. "If I do this, can I see you?"

Lana's thick black hair fell over her face as she shook her head. She rested on his thigh and gazed at the doorway.

"I don't know," she breathed. Sigurd bent over and rested his head on top of hers. Her wings slowly wafted a breeze over them. Drawing warmth from each other only, they fell silent, lost in the implications of what lay ahead.

CHAPTER 24 – RETURN

The weight of his splayed body hung more painfully than it ought to have, mentally laden with the heaviness Sigurd felt in his heart. Watching choppy waves below added to his nausea. The journey back across the seas passed too swiftly, yet seemed to take an age.

The guard fae set him down more gently than they ever had before. Their Queen's instructions not to harm the unpredictable human had been taken seriously. Perhaps it had something to do with their last sight of Lana, stoically standing on the landing balcony with her hair whipping the tears from her face. Never had she looked smaller to them, as fragile, as she had in that parting. The soldiers hoped she never would again, each privately vowing they would push the memory of it away forever. Lest they forget themselves and consider her somehow less fierce and dominating than she could be.

Sigurd stood and rubbed his stiff fingers on his arms. The numbness faded. Patiently waiting, Sigurd asked "Untie" when he was ready. The four stepped forwards and loosened the ropes. Only Uffer did not step back afterwards. Instead, the two men's eyes met. "Look after her," Sigurd said gruffly. Uffer nodded, just once. This human would never again be spoken of. His significance buried.

Sigurd turned and strode off the isolated dune they had alighted upon. In the distance, thin smoke plumes rose lazily into the early evening air. He had some ground to cover and needed to make the most of the remaining daylight.

On his flight, Sigurd had wondered whether he would feel lighter of spirit once on familiar ground again. If being closer to seeing his kinsmen could compensate for the lonely ache in his chest. As he focused on placing one boot in front of another, he acknowledged to himself it had been a foolish hope.

He tried to recall a sense of belonging to his people. Shared bonds built up over years of living together, fighting together and adventuring. But right now, he felt closer to the fae - specifically a fae - than he remembered ever feeling with his own kin. He was nervous about the welcome which awaited him.

He could hear their voices as he drew nearer to the outskirts of the low village complex. An idea dawned on him as the smoke billowed in his direction. The firelight didn't spread too far, especially with the circle of people clustered around it. His kin were relaxing, chatting amiably after their dusk meal. He silently picked his way past the edges of the enclosures, treading on grass rather than the stone littered pathways that could betray his presence too early.

A small face peeked out from under a tent edge in one enclosure. Dark eyes flared, gasping as it caught a glimpse of his silhouette. Sigurd quickly raised his finger to his mouth and winked with a smile. The eyes froze for a moment, then retreated. Sigurd crept onward.

"Askr returns..." he whispered, before pulling himself back into the darkness. He hoped his voice would carry sufficiently. No-one looked around.

"Embla is here..." he called, still quietly but hopefully loud enough to carry.

The voices about the fireside dwindled to a pause.

Sigurd crept a little further; the discussion started up anew. He snuck down the narrow stone passageway marking the entrance to the subterranean homes. Ducking behind the vertical slabs so he remained hidden, he called out again.

"Askr is coming..."

The talk instantly ceased, this time heads turned, searching into the dim.

Sigurd leapt up and roared! A fearsome primordial sound which reverberated across the lowlands. Instantly screams arose from the tents, and men grabbed weapons laid down by their sides. The few women who accompanied them on the voyage brandished plates, ladles or simply fists. Silently focused, they all stood still and searched the dark edges of the settlement, remaining circled with their backs to each other and the fire.

Sigurd casually strolled out of the recessed passageway and clapped. "Great reflexes! Battle ready whenever, wherever!" He laughed, "I'll definitely watch out for that spoon Hilda!" As he walked towards them, he lifted his hands as one might pretend to be a fearsome monster and waggled his fingers at them, grinning all the while.

Collectively, the group relaxed as they recognised their dread-locked friend. Shoulders sagged, a few even laughed.

"Where have you been?"

"You troll! You had us then!"

"We thought you had left to follow Rognval into Valhalla!"

Only Torv approached him to clap him on the back and hug him in welcome. The others hung back, still slightly on edge from his prank. Torv looked into his eyes, searching as the flickering light cast shadows over his face. Then he grinned and led Sigurd over to the log benches gathered around the hearth.

Hilda passed over her mug, "Your throat will be sore after that shout," she said. "What happened to you then this time?"

The crowd laughed. Sigurd chuckled as well, although his hand shook slightly as he drank the warm liquid.

The laughter died down, and they expected a tall tale, a story, from him.

"Is there any stew left?" He asked, delaying.

Torv snorted, "He never gets fed wherever he's been!" They all roared again, slapping their thighs. It was ever the same routine when he reappeared. Sigurd nodded along, half smiling now.

Once a bowl of scraps warmed his hands, Sigurd's nerves calmed. As he slurped the food down as quickly as possible, Torv asked, "Was her cooking as good as my Hilda's?" Hilda laughed and brandished her spoon once more.

"Clearly such a pleasant distraction from us, he didn't care about what was in her other pot," Arvan joked, the edge to his comment offset by a leery wink.

The mental image of Lana bent over a cooking pot,

prompted Sigurd's groin to swell. It also pained him. Sigurd shook his head, "If only you knew..."

He scraped the bowl with a wooden spoon and set it down at his feet. He could feel their expectant eyes watching his every move. Telling stories, fables, myths and songs was as good as entertainment got on a cold night. Using his talent for mime, he loved to bring re-tellings to life. And Sigurd knew his were the best. This story possibly The Best. But even he was worried about how to convince his comrades that this tale was true. Especially as he was muddled about how much of his known belief system could account for what he had experienced.

He lifted his head and stretched his arms up. Looking up into the starry skies above, he thought he saw a glimpse of something. Then he blinked, and it was gone. He smiled and knew news of his safe return would somehow be known to Lana. Encouraged by the prospect, he faced his audience and began.

"I know you have wondered where I went. Perhaps some of you thought I had gone to find Rognval." He shrugged, "I do not deny I considered it. But what happened was far, far stranger."

Sigurd stood and swept his arms wide. "As you know, there are lands where riches and glory are. Lands to raid. Lands to settle - as Rognval wanted us to settle here. But there are also places we should not disturb. Sacred spaces where we, the children of Askr and Embla, are not supposed to go."

Some heads nodded. Torv said, "But not you eh, brother?

Did you think you could discover these other lands on your own? Despite what Rognval asked, you do not want to settle here. We know he forced your into that oath."

Sigurd shook his head. He had hoped to entice his kinsmen into the telling of his story, but it seemed they had other pressing questions to answer first. "True, I did not. I do not. But I made a promise to Rognval."

"A promise you were quick to walk away from!" Arvan said sharply.

Sigurd looked at him.

"An oath you broke within weeks of him passing you the title," the red-headed man continued, standing. "If you cannot take on his responsibilities, commit to his dying request, then you should not expect to be welcomed back as Yarl."

Arvan was more than a few drinks down, but that didn't dissuade him from a challenge. Far from it. A couple of the men close to Arvan clapped encouragement. Sigurd hadn't anticipated a confrontation, but then, he had even not much considered who would step up in leadership in his absence. Now he realised he had made a grave error of judgement.

"Arvan," he placated, "I intended to honour my brother's commands." He turned around on his heels, taking in everyone's eyes. His arms were open, trying to gain their trust once again. "What happened to me prevented that - and will prevent us from honouring his request."

Arvan snorted, throwing his red hair back from his face. "I had no intention of staying in this desolate place. But I will continue here as Yarl, to honour his name if you cannot be trusted to do so."

Sigurd's heart sank. There was probably no avoiding it now. In order to command their respect, he would have to prove his worthiness to carry the title. That meant fighting Arvan - and his most feared sword, Soul-Wrecker. Sigurd knew that Rognval had only managed to keep the experienced warrior on side through a delicate balance of apportioning his raiding profits and allowing him to lead the attack charges.

He tried to stall the inevitable. "It is late, Arvan. I have travelled far this day. Perhaps the decision about what we should do - who should be Yarl - can wait until you have heard where I have been? Of what I have learnt?"

Arvan's eyes narrowed, and he tilted his head to one side, assessing the tall man in front of him. Sigurd knew Arvan could apprise an opponent like no-one else and worried that his recent lack of nourishment showed in his looser clothes. He felt strong enough, but was in no way battle ready - physically or mentally.

"No." Arvan's response took barely any time. The men and women sat around the fireplace began to cheer, raising their fists in the air and shaking them. Soon boots stamped on the ground, thumping out their anticipation. This was the entertainment they wanted, not some vague tale to explain away what was probably yet another meaningless dalliance with a local woman.

CHAPTER 25 – KEEPING PACE

Watching Sigurd lift away had been, Lana thought, the single hardest thing she ever done. The speed at which this had all happened left her with little time to prepare. But, with the Council's threats, she had no choice but to remove Sigurd as soon as possible. Whilst the Council were occupied with replenishing their Lifeforce in the High Hall, Lana had called for the Captain and ordered Sigurd's return to his people.

She returned to her chambers feeling broken inside. But to anyone who saw her, she hoped she presented as her usual self, in control. The facade hid the truth she was only just starting to understand. Not only was Sigurd the last and only hope she had of entreating the native humans to return to the ceremonies, he was also the only person who had ever made her feel. The idea of his death, his complete absence forever, made her stomach and heart clench so tightly she could barely draw breath. She pushed the thought away as quickly as it had entered.

She sat on the bed, fidgeting with her fingernails. Besides, if the Council found out there had been a human prisoner who had then died under Naturae's watch, that would be worse surely? Even though he was, to the fae and the humans they had dominion over, an invader. Whether she liked it or not, times had changed and the activities of the Sation wars were no longer acceptable under the treaty. It had come down to losing her throne or, she feared, her life, if she failed to act.

Unable to help herself, Lana went to the window, just in case there was a last remaining glimpse of him. Her heart thumped as she contemplated flying after him, only for one final touch. A quick pull of his essence. Aching with the battle of head over heart, Lana tore herself away from the view over the treetops. The sky would turn red before long and that colour always irked her. She couldn't face it right now.

She returned to sitting on the edge of her bed. Her fingers automatically smoothed down the coverlet. Repetitively stroking the ripples down, the slight roughness of the woven fabric comforting her.

Unbidden, the memory of touching Sigurd through his tunic rose into her mind. She tried to push it away by blinking, like she had other thoughts of him. But it was a stubborn reminder, rising in her with panic. She could never see him again, never touch him. Her lip wobbled, despite her pressing them together.

Lana stood and flapped her wings. Pacing would help. She began to walk. Tried to focus on the route she knew so well. Step step step, turn, ten steps to the door, turn, twelve steps along, turn. Around the bed, turn, step step, turn. The rhythm of it usually calmed her, but not today. Faster and faster she walked. Wing flap with each turn she made. Around and around. Each item was in its place.

Deliberately she avoided looking out of the window as she passed it on her circuit. The well-worn floorboards beneath her feet felt smooth and began to warm as she continued along the routine.

After some time, she began to feel a little calmer. She carried on walking though, measuring the familiar sensations underfoot and the blank walls around her chambers. She also avoided looking at the desk in the centre of the room. Although tidy, it was a reminder of her responsibilities to the Queendom. The one thing she was trying to save by sending Sigurd away. Better to avoid thinking about it.

Outside, the sky transitioned through its hated sunset into darkness. She paced some more, her feet now aching from the walking.

The next time she reached the bed, Lana slowed. Inwardly checking with herself that she was sufficiently tired enough to stop, she walked around to the other side with slower steps. Yes...she could rest. She pulled herself onto the soft covers and stretched out. Staring above at the ceiling, counting the way around the pale spokes that formed the roof supports. A never ending rotation, round and around until her eyelids dropped.

CHAPTER 26 - YARL

Sigurd looked at Arvan across the fire. The flames flickered, highlighting his craggy face and the deep red streaks of his hair.

A warrior in his prime, Sigurd had no desire to fight his friend. For the other menfolk they travelled with, this was a matter of honour. Who to follow. Who to believe in. There was no escaping it.

Looking around the crowd, Sigurd stood and slowly circled the fireplace. Arvan unsheathed Soul Wrecker and leaned on the hilt, watching. There were plenty of weapons propped against the seating logs or sheathed and held on belts. But he wanted his own. If he were going to die, here and now, it would be with Gramr in his hands. He needed all the fierce he could get; only Gramr would do.

"What have you done with Gramr?" Sigurd asked of Torv. Surely he would have taken care of his weapon for him? Torv's eyes shifted over to a younger man, a recruit who had joined their journey from a village far away in their homelands. Sigurd recalled he had committed himself to Rognval's service only days before they left, he couldn't even remember how the youngster had fought when they landed. He was barely more than a boy.

"He needed a blade," Torv shrugged. "His shattered."

Cheap and poorly crafted weaponry - a hallmark of a low-born. One could only afford to trade for better after gaining experience and wealth from raiding. Sigurd nodded at the boy who reached behind him and reluctantly handed up the weapon. Unsheathing the glinting blade, Sigurd smiled. The lad had cleaned and sharpened his new possession with a pride he himself once felt over owning such a sword.

"I'll fight you, if that's what you want, Arvan," Sigurd said, turning towards him. "But understand - this is not the pathway to gold or glory."

Arvan grunted, "Glory?" He spat on the ground. "It is not for glory that I challenge you."

"Then why?"

Arvan's mouth lifted, just a hint on one side. "You cannot command the respect of us if you cannot deliver on a simple promise."

"It was not a simple promise. Nor was it one you wanted to follow through on either."

Arvan shrugged. "But I have. I stepped up when they asked me not to return. I fought for it and took the responsibility when you abandoned us. For that, I am Yarl now."

Sigurd glanced around the crowd. Some were shaking their heads, but others stared at the ground as if it would offer them an alternative. Arvan was not known for his consideration of others' feelings. It was likely that his rule here was enforced by commands and fear, rather than persuasion and historic respect for a family of leaders.

Gesturing over to a patch of grass beyond the gathering,

"There is no need to endanger others - we have plenty of space," Sigurd said.

Arvan removed his fur throw and unkinked his neck and shoulders, before moving away from the warmth of the fire. Sigurd, having no additional layers to hinder his movement, flexed Gramr. The familiar weight of his blade comforted him. Thankfully, the boy hadn't replaced the worn thongs wrapped for grip around the hilt.

He jumped over a log, and then stood, legs lowered, sword up, facing Arvan.

"I warn you, you are about to die," Sigurd threatened.

Arvan curled his lip again. Their eyes met through the low light. A flash of reluctance passed between them before Arvan's steeled over with resolve.

Their friends, kinsmen and family shuffled around to watch. Some ran around to the other side of the wide flat stretch and stood on dunes to get a better view. As the two men appraised each other, flaming torches, spitting with seal fat, were lit and stuck in the ground to illuminate the action. Anticipation, mixed with no small amount of ambivalence, filled the night air.

Sigurd had chosen to move the fight away from the closely packed fireside not because of the risk of hurting others, but because he knew his strength in battle was his nimble footwork. Arvan, bulky and muscled, carried the weight of experience and training well. He was a formidable opponent - who Sigurd had fought side by side with on many an occasion. Sigurd, taller and slimmer, hoped that his reflexes would enable him to dodge the hefty thrusts and lunges which would no doubt rain down on him.

Warily they circled each other, both testing the firmness of the ground as they silently tried to plan how to out-manoeuvre each other. There was no point in wasting energy with tentative jabs or mis-judged lunges. Both men knew the other's capabilities too well. Both believed they could win.

The crowd, beginning to get bored with the prowling, wanted action. Feet began to thump, chanting started. Sigurd was relieved thus far the calls didn't seem to suggest a preference for the winner. No names, just a low throb of indistinguishable sounds to add to the tension.

"To first blood?" Sigurd offered.

Slowly, Arvan shook his head. Never wavering eyes watched Sigurd for a tell. Sigurd swallowed – it had been worth a try.

Arvan leaned onto his back foot, signalling to Sigurd he was about to attack. Soul Wrecker dipped, then swooped up behind Arvan. Sigurd quickly raised his shorter but wider Gramr and blocked the brutal downward strike that betrayed Arvan's desire. The clash of metal resulted in a collective intake of breath, followed by a cheer. The blades slid away, although the ringing shock wave lingered in Sigurd's arm.

Breathing in as he repositioned his sword, Sigurd spun on his heel, briefly exposing his back, to bring Gramr low and fast. Arvan anticipated this balletic move and had already positioned Soul Wrecker to deflect. The clang reverberated through the night air.

Shifting his weight forwards, Arvan pushed his blade upwards, moving Soul Wrecker's tip between Sigurd's legs.

Sigurd felt the strain in his wrist as he resisted, pushing down on the blades. There was no time to reposition his sword, so Sigurd lent fully back on his right leg and spun as he kicked out at Arvan. The larger man barely moved as the muscled bulk of his torso absorbed the blow.

As Sigurd shuffled quickly to create space, the jolting agony of a hilt came down hard on his shoulder, sending him sprawling to the ground. Dust filled his mouth as his face hit the dirt, but he rolled away, swiftly rising to his feet in one graceful move.

Thankful for the distance between them, Sigurd spat the soil from his mouth, never taking his eyes off Arvan as they wheeled around each other. He flexed and rotated his sore shoulder and back, noting that the crowd had fallen silent.

Sigurd flicked Gramr over in a circle. Reminding Arvan with a nimble move of his perfectly balanced blade that he had still had more to prove.

Taking no notice, Arvan's hulk charged at him, roaring with Soul Wrecker raised. Sigurd ducked his lithe frame to one side. The sword whispered as it swooped close to his arm. Arvan's body lunged past him - once in transit, hard to stop. The tip of Soul Wrecker hit the ground, slightly embedding with the impact.

Sigurd wheeled around again, crouching low as he rotated. Sharp and clean, Gramr sliced the back of Arvan's calf through the leather.

Another rage-filled cry came from Arvan's mouth, terrifying the people standing closest.

The nick was not enough to stop him in his tracks, but just

enough. First blood.

Sigurd stepped backwards, Gramr still held in front of him. Would Arvan stop now? The red-head wheeled around and glared. Through his fury, would he recognise what Sigurd already knew: their fighting styles were complimentary on a battlefield, but brute strength was only effective if the enemy was unprepared for it. Sigurd could dodge a charge too easily. Arvan would have to be smarter than that.

Sigurd pulled Gramr back with a bent arm held close to his head and weighted himself into his knees. Holding his other arm out for perfect balance, he was ready to strike.

"Enough!" called out Torv. "First blood has been struck."

Arvan's head whipped around, still seeing red. Snapping to focus on Sigurd, waiting.

With pleading eyes, Sigurd said, "Brother, we are too few as it is."

Arvan snarled. "To the death."

Sigurd swallowed but held his pose while Arvan stepped closer. Not a flicker of pain crossed his face as he weighted his bleeding calf. Arvan wheeled his sword around - in his hands it looked almost weightless, but Sigurd knew the sword well. Knew that wrist-wielding it for any period of time would make it feel heavy very quickly. It was his only hope.

Stepping forward himself, Sigurd parried Gramr in a move which Arvan could easily deflect and re parry. Their two bodies drew closer. Deliberately Sigurd kept advancing, which reduced the ability for Arvan to strike fully with the full force of his arm. Clash and parry. Swipe and deflect. They danced with steel, face to face, breath to hot breath.

They were too similar in a duelling match, Sigurd thought. Arvan and he had trained together as boys; at close quarters they were very evenly matched. But Gramr was designed for close combat - her wide blade perfect for sliding between ribs through a shield wall. She was an unusual combination of short sword and long seax, perfectly balanced. Sigurd couldn't risk stepping back, giving Arvan room to fully swing Soul Wrecker.

Sigurd kept his advance going, pushing pushing all the while. Making Arvan work on that sore calf. Forcing him to lift and defend with an unwieldy close combat weapon.

Sigurd felt the ground beneath him, dry from the sun, become uneven as boots pushed up the mud. Clang, retreat, pause. Different angle, clash, push off. Their blades flew at each other faster, catching the light of the torches. Fiercely concentrating on not missing a beat. The danger of a lull - it opened up an opportunity to the other.

Arvan was obviously thinking the same, as he quickly stepped backward, dropped Soul Wrecker to the earth and shoulder-charged Sigurd's middle. Sigurd could only bring the hilt of Gramr down on Arvan's ribs, and not with as much force as he would have liked.

He kept hold of the blade though as Arvan dug his toes in and pushed his bulk forwards. Losing his balance, Sigurd fell backwards to the ground. Arvan sat on Sigurd's chest, then balled his fists, pulled back and swiped a momentous blow to Sigurd's half ear. Pinned down and winded, Sigurd's head reeled from the impact.

Arvan leaned in closer. Smelling the sweat emanating

from him, Sigurd's eyes lolled back into his head. A sense of unease accompanied the ragged breath he drew in through his nostrils.

Out of nowhere, another blow to his jaw, knocking his head to the other side of the ground. Sigurd's teeth clacked together with the force. His hand almost let go of Gramr. Tasting blood, Sigurd tried to wriggle out from the weight on top of him, before another punch could land. Arvan drew his body up and retracted his arm, preparing for the knockout blow.

Sigurd felt the shifting weight and realised he was still holding his lucky short blade. He spun the weapon and stabbed into the space between Arvan's hips and ribs. Silky smooth, the blade sank deep as Sigurd pushed with his remaining strength.

Arvan let out a deep and horrible gasp. Almost immediately, blood bubbled out from his mouth as his internals punctured. He coughed. Sigurd's eyes flared as his friend arched his back - unwittingly driving Gramr deeper. Weight increased on Sigurd's chest as thigh muscles rebelled and clenched, and Arvan tried to wrench himself free. Finally, Arvan's torso crumpled and collapsed, directly on top of Sigurd's head.

For a moment Sigurd froze - stunned by what had just happened. Although he wanted to breathe, this was the last time he would feel the warm embrace of his friend. His brother in arms. He hadn't wanted this end for him.

Sigurd pushed Arvan off him. Although there were shouts and cheers in the background, he did not hear them. Crawling in the dirt, half blind with Arvan's blood and spittle, he searched for Soul Wrecker. He felt a hand on his shoulder but shrugged it off. Patting the earth as he moved around, tears mingling with the red spattered across his face. He finally felt the cold metal and grabbed it. The blade slit his finger a little, but it was a small price to pay.

He shuffled back to Arvan and closed the warrior's hands around the hilt. Then he sat back on his heels and let the waters of regret flow. Hoping it wasn't too late for Soul Wrecker to guide her owner to Valhalla after all.

CHAPTER 27 - WITHDRAWL

When Lana sluggishly awoke the next morning, her first thought was of Sigurd. Sitting bolt upright, her chest felt tight and heavy. She breathed out fully, trying to release it but failing miserably. In, out, in, out. The pain did not dissipate. She collapsed back onto the bed and stared at the spokes above her. Her heart pounded. Her mouth felt dry.

He was gone.

She gnawed her lip, her mind turning over. Some small part of her wished that Tolant would come in and remind her of all the duties she was supposed to undertake. Anything to distract her. Then she remembered - Tolant was in the Beneath, awaiting her judgment on what to do with him.

With a sigh, Lana closed her eyes. The pressure on her chest deepened. Tolant's betrayal disappointed her more than she had previously given thought to. Now, she had made the decision to send away the only other person who gave her routine and comfort. However, he had betrayed her, of that she was in no doubts. He could never be trusted again.

She was alone.

She turned her head to the pillow and drew her legs up, curling into a ball. Why had she let herself get into this state, she questioned? Angry though she was with Tolant, he had been right. She should have stayed apart from the human.

Getting close to him had only caused her pain. Sigurd had opened up her heart to feelings, which now were hurting.

There was no going back. She knew now what it was to laugh freely, touch, and feel. How did one stop wanting those things, once they were known?

She recognised another, more familiar emotion, building. Anger. She began to think about all the things she disliked in an effort to fuel the ire. Fury, she knew about. Fury blinded out all the other feelings which were so unwelcome. Her mouth tightened. Mentally, she pulled out the frustrations of her situation. Focused on the things which were beyond her control. Sigurd instantly sprang back, insistent. Lana recalled her impressions when they first met. His strangeness. His violence. His unpredictability. His total disregard for who she was and what she was.

Yes, the more Lana thought about it, the longer the list grew. His mocking of her. Embarrassing her. He was the one who invaded - not just her dominion, but herself. He was nothing more than a rogue who took what he wanted and left behind devastation.

She had been right to send him away.

She should have done it sooner. In fact, Tolant - wretch that he was, had been correct. She shouldn't have let him see anything of Naturae, of her. She should have kept him at arm's length, then killed him. Destroyed the evidence. He knew nothing. Had provided no useful information after all.

Her anger mounted, and before she knew it, Lana found herself upright and pacing again. Her face twisted into a tight wall of tension. Sigurd was to blame. She recognised she was also cross with herself, but that didn't matter. He was the cause of the pain. It was better that he wasn't here in person, otherwise she didn't know what she would do to vent this pressure.

She pulled on a fresh gown, almost tearing the seams as she hastily dressed. Wrenched open the door and flew out. The door banged behind her on its hinges, a warning to anyone of her vile mood. Straight down the hallway, snarling at workers who dared to peep out from the branched corridors. Wings flapping purposefully hard caused a down-draft in her wake. Out the double doors, through the atrium, then outside into the late summer sunshine. Even that irritated her - the weather ought to be dark and cloudy to match her mood. She landed in the clearing, fists clenched.

"Captain!" Lana shouted. Waited a few seconds; her heart thumping uncomfortably against in her chest. "Captain! Get out here!"

His doorway flew open and a brown-haired head poked out. The soldier called back into the room, then retracted inside, leaving the door ajar. After a moment, the Captain calmly and properly appeared. He walked over to the Queen and bowed, holding his face deliberately blank. With the Queen so clearly in a rage, it was best to let her dictate what action was required. Never let her see what you felt, she didn't care.

"I require daily updates on the activities of the human you have returned to his people," Lana snapped.

The Captain stood and nodded once. Never question, he told himself.

"Full surveillance at all times. The spy, Issam, is to stay within their village and provide verbal reports to be passed to one of your soldiers daily. I need to know exactly what that human," Lana almost spat, "is telling the islanders to do."

Another nod. The Captain didn't trust himself to speak; anything could trigger an attack when the Queen was like this and he didn't choose to be on the receiving end of it. He had no idea how Issam was supposed to ingratiate himself into the already upset village for an extended period of time, but the spy was resourceful enough.

Lana's mouth tightened. She glared at the Captain, "I want to know everything. Report directly to me. Everything!"

Shaking his head up and down, "Yes, your Highness. I will instruct the spy and guards right now." He turned to leave, but the Queen stopped him with a question and narrowed eyes.

"Tolant, he remains in the Beneath?"

The Captain briefly wondered whether she was actually going to enquire after another person's well-being. Then he realised she simply didn't trust him, or his soldiers. He had heard rumours about what happened, but his guards were very specific in that the Queen had ordered - in full view of the most senior Fae there were -that her closest Advisor be locked away. Carefully, he reassured, "He is, your Highness. Are there any special instructions for him?"

There was a pause before she snapped, "No. Keep him there. No-one is to have access. No-one is to go near enough to even hear his deceitful tongue."

At some point Lana knew she would need to make a

decision about her advisor. But without anyone else to turn to for support, she was not certain about what she ought to do about him. There was plenty of time to decide, he wasn't going anywhere.

CHAPTER 28 - BUILDING BRIDGES

Overnight, soft mists rolled in across the land. Morning brought with it a painful awakening. When Sigurd stumbled out of the dwelling he had retreated into last night, the same hovel which he previously inhabited, and emerged into the grey light, he wondered if the fog was Lana's doing. He was still not entirely sure that he believed her when she told him the mists of Naturae were not her creation. Still wondered at what kind of powers she possessed. Gud or not a gud. There was so much he yet wanted to find out about her - would he ever get the chance now?

The damp fog droplets peppering his face reminded him of his commitment to her. His promise to her conflicted with the pledge he had made to Rognval. So which was the right path?

He sighed and rubbed his whiskers as he looked around. Already people were working through the chill of the late summer morning - tending to livestock, tidying the remnants of last night's meal away. Through the greyness, he could hear the call of gulls chattering to each other. Strange, he had not heard birdsong on Naturae. Perhaps they knew other - maybe superior - flying beasts had staked their claim to that land.

Staking a claim - a moment of clarity struck him: the

assertion of dominance had led up to this point. If they, Rognval and himself, hadn't arrived on these shores, none of this would have happened. Rognval would be alive. As would Arvan. Sigurd ran his hand over his shoulder. The bruise would be showing by now. A temporary reminder of the deadly stakes that making a claim had caused. His chest felt heavy at the thought of it.

The mood around the fireside last night had fallen quiet as soon as he had killed Arvan. There had been no victory cheers, claps on the back. Just sorrow that another of their number had died. Acceptance of his return to leadership marked more by respecting his space to grieve, than any other fealty gestures. Even though he had been nominally in charge of them for only a short time after Rognval's death, his people knew him and knew what to expect of his command.

Which wasn't much, he acknowledged to himself now. The mist blocking his view of the horizon adequately reflected how his earlier attempts at decision making had gone. Fuddled and blind. He hadn't given enough thought to how he was going to manage his missions either. The fog in front of him didn't bode well.

Reluctantly, Sigurd first faced the enormous problem of how to convince the Northmen (and women) to leave. Sail away from fertile lands and profitable slaves with nothing to show for their efforts. He hadn't had a plan last night - it had all happened so quickly. But now, he realised he needed more than a story. He needed a better plan.

Sigurd walked over to a huge bladder hanging next to the entrance to the houses. He loosened the thong which held the spout closed and poured spring water straight into his mouth. The brackish taste reminded him of Naturae, and that first drink after his near-death illness. In his heart, he acknowledged his yearning to be back with Lana. Although it had been made abundantly clear that he was in Naturae against his own free will, somehow the lack of responsibility for others had been liberating. As he saw it, the only person he answered to was Lana. Their time together had been a joy, not a chore. Even though it had been exhausting.

Pouring more cold water over his face, he scrubbed it with his sleeve and rinsed his mouth out. Then, he walked over to where the islanders, prisoners really, were being held. As he approached the high woven fences, it occurred to him that immediate changes were required. For one, keeping people penned in like cattle served little purpose on a small island. Back home, where the never-ending craggy landscape made escape possible, having slaves locked up was usual. But here it merely kept them corralled for when you wanted to order them to do something. They hadn't brought enough chains with them to have everyone permanently imprisoned. Workers needed freedom to be able to gather crops, so sword points and shouting were used instead keep them under control.

Common sense told him that, even in this flat landscape, the villagers would know that survival depended on each person playing their part in harvesting sufficient food, combustible materials and drinks to last through the winter. Although Sigurd suspected that the islands' southerly aspect meant winters were not quite as harsh as they were back home, that didn't mean precautions shouldn't be taken, stockpiles created. He wondered how bad the weather would get here. Their homes were almost under the ground, which surely suggested they needed the earth's protection from the winds at least, if not the temperature?

And where could the villagers run off to? Having been flown for hours over the sea, he knew it was not possible to make the journey to other islands without a boat. So, the obvious conclusion was to remove the ability to cross water. Or rather, strictly curtail access to the vessels instead. However, there was also fish to be caught here, which added to the winter supplies. He liked smoked fish, perhaps they made the same here to preserve it?

He shook his head. How foolish he had been not to have seen it before. There was so much to discuss with the islanders. Information he required of them for his plan to succeed. He hoped the language he had learnt in Naturae was similar enough for him to communicate his questions. Time to find out.

"Hello," he cheerfully hailed the grubby-looking villagers. A few dull eyes looked up at him. Sigurd tried again, smiling as he unlocked the gate and entered the enclosure. Still, a wary and silent response. He stood there and assessed the group. Huddled together for warmth, their thin clothes damp through from the dew and mist. The sail strung overhead in the corner of the pen provided no protection, and autumn would soon be setting in.

"Food?" One of the children asked and held out a hand. The same feisty boy who Rognval had commended after the first raid. Of course! With an inward sigh of relief that he recognised the word, Sigurd slapped his head, and rubbed his stomach, hoping it would gurgle on cue. It didn't, but the message was received and the child tentatively lifted his lips in hope.

Sigurd beckoned them. "Come! Have food. Eat and get warm," he said, in Lana's language. Some of them got to their feet, slightly surprised at being spoken to in something resembling words that they knew, then looked back at the people still lying prone on the ground. Three inert bodies were huddled under coarsely woven sackcloths.

Recalling that some of the villagers had sustained injuries during their attack, Sigurd felt a wave of regret. Had things followed their usual pattern, the injured men might have been taken as prisoners back to the homeland. If they survived the journey, the healers would treat them before they were sold on. Here, they had limited medicinal resources.

Sigurd thought about what else he could do as he led them over to the outside fireplace. Like it or not, these people were under his care now. They had been before, but in truth, he had been too bogged down with grief and sudden leadership burdens to really consider a plan for their future. Part of him was surprised that Arvan hadn't sent them back with one of the ships to sell. Now he needed to think about the practicalities of over-wintering and slave ownership.

There were fifteen villagers trailing suspiciously behind him, he counted. He knew the his men would have dragged some others out to labour, so perhaps about twenty in total. The Northmen and their wives themselves numbered triple that. And then there were the other island inhabitants, taken from the first few raids. All told, he estimated there were probably over a hundred mouths to feed. And this was not a large island.

Sigurd began to pile a few nearby branches on the still warm embers from last night. He blew low, encouraging the flames to flicker up and catch. One of the women collected a few of the dried peat bricks stacked at the side of the house wall slabs and banked the fire. They jostled around the small but growing flames, rubbing their hands together.

Trusting their need to get warm would override their desire to run, Sigurd jogged over and called down into the housing complex. "Who is here to bring food?"

Hilda's blonde head poked out. "Who's asking?" She joked. "Oh, you're up then I see!"

She came towards the entrance, little feet making tiny squelches on the damp pathway. Overnight, the mist had condensed, seeped down through the overhead slabs which provided cover to the dark network of passages between houses. Sigurd stood and pointed at the group of villagers. "I need to talk to them, and they require something in their bellies."

She raised an eyebrow.

"Please."

Hilda nodded. She was slightly younger than Sigurd's own mother but assumed a maternal manner with all the menfolk she travelled with. She was frequently the designated supplier of prisoners' food and often took charge of catering when the occasion required a larger feast. No-one could roast a goat like Hilda. Even though Northmen could cook quite well for themselves, a hot meal prepared by someone else was guaranteed to raise the spirits of even the most battle weary of warriors. Torv's wife was therefore one of the most protected people they sailed with, although as a former shield maiden she was perfectly capable of wielding a weapon herself.

"I've a pot of mashed grains I was making ready for tomorrow," she said. "I'll bring it out."

Sigurd beamed at her.

"What are you wanting to talk about with them, anyway? They can't understand what we say. What's the point?"

"I have learnt a little of what I hope is their language whilst I was..." Sigurd paused, preferring not to ruin the story he had planned to tell them all later. "Away."

His eyes begged for her not to push him on this.

Hilda turned and retreated into the passage. He was always a bit odd, that Sigurd, she thought. One never knew what he was going to do next. It was a little unsettling. Charming, funny, but unreliable nonetheless. At least he wasn't bossy like Arvan. She wasn't sorry to see him fall, hot-headed brute.

Sigurd ambled back to the communal fireplace. Chilly and wary, the islanders were warming themselves, holding damp tunics towards the smoky flames to dry. He slowed his pace, hoping to catch snatches of conversation amongst them.

The villagers fell quiet though, spotting his lanky frame emerging. Sigurd took a seat on a vacant log close to the fire and rubbed his hands. Not long afterwards, just as people shuffled around, seating themselves and wondering what was about to happen, Hilda arrived. The vat swinging from the crook of her arm was heavy; her face red from exertion over slippery stones. A middle-aged woman approached to help her. They exchanged wary smiles and began to ladle out some bowlfuls.

The mashed grains were cool enough that they could be scooped and stuffed into hungry mouths quickly. No-one bothered to rinse their dirty hands, Sigurd noticed. A sign that they had been pitifully short on meals. He ate his portion slowly. Although bland, the mash was creamy and filling. He savoured cooked food now, the diet of raw meat and leaves hadn't really tempted him as much as home cooking. Even though his usual fare during winter was an assortment of pickled meats, salted or dried fish and blood-loaves, he liked the warmth of a cooked meal. It soothed the stomach to digest also.

Sigurd waited until the point of licking the bowls before he tried to talk again.

"Good food," he said tentatively, watching their reaction. Slightly brighter eyes flew up to meet his blue ones. "Eat! Have more," he offered. Hilda was ready with her ladle. As the children approached, he saw their bellies were already protruding. He rubbed his own, saying, "Need more to grow strong! Like me!" He raised a bicep.

Their faces fell again. Perhaps demonstrating one's strength wasn't appropriate, Sigurd realised. These people had lost much to their superior warrior physique, he supposed. He stood up and bared his hands.

"I am sorry," he began, gesturing around at their village

and then their new 'home'. It was clearly not what the villagers were expecting him to say, but his recent experiences had taught him a valuable lesson about imprisonment. That they understood him at all caught Hilda by surprise as well.

"I need to talk to you about the future." Sigurd tried to meet as many eyes as he could, so they would heed his earnest request.

One of the older men, his white hair hanging in rat's tails about his face, spoke up. "It is not enough to apologise." He looked around at his family and friends, then up at the tall invader. "You need to go, leave us in peace."

Sigurd struggled to make out the man's thick accent but understood sufficiently to infer what the quietly spoken elder was saying. He nodded, shot a glance at Hilda then said, "We will."

When the villagers began to talk rapidly amongst themselves, Hilda glared at Sigurd. She wasn't sure, but whatever their Yarl had just told them was clearly welcome news.

"You need go back to your honouring." Sigurd interrupted, waving his arm out towards the farmland behind them. "Go back to ritual. Ceremony."

The elder frowned. "Why do you care what we do?"

"I don't," Sigurd responded. "But it is important you honour *your* Guds."

He breathed out, hoping that he had achieved what Lana required of him. In part, at least. He watched as the villagers began to talk amongst themselves, wishing they would take this offer in the spirit in which it was intended. He was himself curious about their rituals, especially now he had an understanding of who they were worshipping.

Hilda's eyebrows knitted together. She understood the word Gud. What had this man been up to, she wondered? She clutched her small silver hammer and sent a quick prayer over. Sighing, she picked up the cauldron and retreated to the houses once more.

CHAPTER 29 – A MESSAGE

Sigurd left the native Orkneans by the fire. He instructed the late-rising lad who had cared for Gramr to watch over them, but not with threats of violence. Gier happily agreed, keen to show his acceptance of Sigurd's return to leadership. So he sat close to them, watching and nursing his sore head. Last night's commiserations at losing a precious object and Arvan sinking in.

Sigurd had shared a meaningful glance with the confident elder before he walked away. Fairly secure in the knowledge that his directive would be discussed at length, he was attempting to demonstrate his trust in the group by leaving them relatively unattended. That trust didn't extend far just yet though. The boats needed securing, so that escape was prevented. The lack of fishing as a result was a worry for later.

The beach was clearing of mists by the time he reached it. The sun was slow to penetrate but making headway as the day progressed. Sigurd checked their own vessels first, now pulled securely up onto the sand, almost filling the small cove. He wondered again why no-one had returned with the spoils of their raids before, leaving those who intended to settle here behind. Their loyalty to Rognval's last request was stronger than he himself had felt. But it surprised him Arvan had also remained. Perhaps it was the lure of leadership which had kept him here, the opportunity to mould a settlement and rule too tempting.

Their beached boats yielded a surprise, however. Someone was huddled against the side, almost under the tall gunwale of his Thora. Wearing baggy knitted clothing, and a cape loosely draped for extra warmth, a pale face hinted at fear and chill. Sigurd didn't recognise him, although there was something familiar about the cast to his narrow face. He crouched down beside him and smiled. "Where are you supposed to be?" He asked in their tongue.

For a moment, the young man looked away, confused. Sigurd frowned. Then the boy held up a pair of fish, wrapped in a net. Sigurd thought he understood, so gripped him by a scruff of clothing and hauled him upright.

"There is no need to steal now," he explained. "We must all work together to eat."

The young man's eyebrows knitted together. Sigurd searched his face for some kind of recognition that his words were being comprehended but, surprisingly, dark eyes examined him back with a confidence that the other villagers lacked. He pushed the man towards the dunes and pointed. "Go, join the others."

The lad dithered for a moment, then looked at his fish before moving off. Sigurd shook his head with a smile, sure that the reason for the man's confusion was his own unexpected reasonableness. It didn't occur to him to ask how he had got the fish.

Sigurd carried on up the beach and started to examine the

islanders' fishing boats. His men had already broken one of them up, its mast hacked down close to the hull. Oars, being too short to use on their own ships, removed, probably used as firewood. The sail had been re-purposed as the cover on the outside enclosures. The two other smaller vessels were also lacking oars and sails.

No-one would be escaping in them. No-one could fish for a while either. They hadn't yet been smashed up for firewood, but over time that was inevitable.

Was that going to be an issue, Sigurd mused? How much fish did it take to supplement their diets? Quite a lot, he suspected, as he carried on past the boats and around the cove. Their own ships were not designed as fishing vessels, although they could be, he considered. But they needed a number of people to crew them, unlike the smaller crafts the islanders used. The knarrs which they sailed here in were too large for just a few bodies to furtively push them out into the shallows, thankfully. With a nod of satisfaction, he decided he wasn't too concerned about escape any more.

To be able to use the fishing boats, they would need replacement wood. Few trees grew on this island, except in the dips. This posed a challenge and explained why their houses were built out of stone, Sigurd realised. Furthermore, the Northmen hadn't yet fully got to grips with the processes for the main fuel here - the peat underground. He would have to learn the technique, and soon. The brick stockpile that the woman banked the fire from earlier looked too low to last a winter. He didn't fancy digging out frozen earth in the wind which he suspected would add more chill!

Sigurd gazed out to sea, climbing a little on the slabs of algae-covered rocks which edged the beach. He checked above - not even a gull in the sky. Although this wasn't the same place as they had snatched him from, it wasn't that far away. Equally, he knew Lana wanted him here, needed him here, to carry out her request. Order. Demand. However you phrased it, he didn't, in his soul, believe she wouldn't send for him again. No matter how much he craved seeing her. Holding her. He sighed, forcing his mind to concentrate on the immediate task at hand. Not bow to the tight pressure, the yearning for her presence, which had silently accompanied him since he left Naturae.

A glimpse of a horizon lay ahead, hazily coming into view through the dispersing mist. Not far from the shore, clusters of seaweed topped rocks exposed by the retreating tide. Seals had begun to flop up onto them to rest. With limpid brown eyes, they watched the beach and sea, their casual stance belying their vigilance. Sigurd's mouth filled with saliva, remembering the juicy and tasty meat they provided. If one could catch a seal of course - slippery, watchful and smart, they were not the easiest of prey to hunt.

An unfamiliar feeling of pride in himself grew as he surveyed the still grey skies again. Surprise, as well. Not a day ago, he had been a virtual prisoner, albeit in the company of a wondrous Queen. And here he was, considering the long-term planning required to ensure the survival of not only his kin, but their newly freed slaves. He barely recognised himself. In his heart, he felt Rognval and Lana would also be proud of him. They would approve of, if not of all, some of the progress he had made.

That is not to say, he acknowledged, that this achievement was not tinged by sadness; the death of Arvan, by his own hand, had been necessary. His lips clenched together as he offered up a silent prayer to Thor. It would have been preferable to have Arvan's strength with them here, rather than feasting in Valhalla with Rognval. Preferable to have them both here. A seal yawned at him, as if to say, get over yourself, get on with it.

Sigurd turned back to the beach and walked down to the water's edge. A pebble rattled up on the surf to his feet, almost identical to the stone Lana had used when they marked in the sand. Picking it up, he walked midway between the waves and the boats and began to scrawl in the flat grit.

'Lana' he wrote first, remembering the beautiful swirls her name formed in Faelore. Then he drew the runes for his own name. Standing back to admire his handiwork, he smiled. Then he bent down and dragged a wide circle around both sets of markings. He knew the evening tide would wash them away, but the waters which joined their islands were connected. Somehow, he wished his message, his declaration of love, would reach her.

CHAPTER 30 - DEADLY REUNION

Lana woke up sweating. After a few days of internal argument, pacing the floor of her chambers to the point of exhaustion, she had slept finally. Despite the previous night's efforts trying to ignore her constant cravings for Sigurd, morning had somehow arrived and almost immediately, she wished that it hadn't. It was such a revolting feeling - the crawling underneath her skin completely at odds with the sensations Sigurd had provoked within her from his touch. Her mouth dry. Heart thumping. Yet she knew the feelings had the same source. Him. Today, utterly fed up with her own helplessness, Lana was spurred into action.

She left from her window, so the guards outside her doorway wouldn't see. It was so early in the morning, the sea was still drawing into the shore. Flying as fast as she could through the dawn light towards Rousay, the crawling sensation was tempered only by the rush of cool air brushing over her body. Hope for a release urging her to beat her wings faster. This rash act would surely be condemned, were anyone to know where she was going. But who would notice her absence, other than the worker fae who tended her chambers daily?

She wasn't sure what had provoked her into action this time, having endured the same extreme reactions within her body every day since Sigurd had gone. Perhaps it was the dawning realisation that the cycle needed to be broken. Yesterday in the Pupaetory, Lana had sat amongst the leaves, crooning to the tiny pods dangling from the branches. The yellowing colour of the vine worried her - it seemed, like the others, it was dying out. The chrysalis looked dry and stunted, although she had done her best to bless them with the little Lifeforce she gained from Sigurd before he left. Not even recalling memories of their time together produced ribbons. So why did she still feel this ache? And this rage?

Perhaps the prompt to move was the lack of communication, despite ordering the Captain to send kestrels to Issam for an update. The not knowing where he was ate at her almost as much as the yearning for him. He should have gone by now, back to his people. Returned to tell them not to come this way west any more.

Patience had never been her strong suit. Until this morning, she had vacillated between duty, anger and pain. Restraining herself whilst needing to exhaust herself in order to rest. The peculiar combination of longing and loathing that Sigurd left her with had put her in this position - imprisoning her with indecision.

Who was she fooling? This wasn't about needing information. She needed him. All anger dissipated as soon as she accepted this to herself. She. Needed. Him.

So she flew. Her eyes began to scour the seas below. She had a wider view the higher she was, but kept dipping down below cloud level in case she missed something. Unsure of her own reactions were she to see him. Uncertain on if he would even be there still. Driven on by desperation, Lana cleared her mind and tried not to think about what she would do next. Not try to second guess a man she knew to be entirely undependable, not to mention unpredictable. At least she would know more than she did right now. One way or another.

*****

Although he had barely slept, Sigurd was awake and on the beach. It had become his private routine since returning - to carve out his little love runes in the sand as the morning tide receded. It bothered him in these moments, that he still had not managed to find a way of warning his fellow Northmen that they needed to leave and never return. Their questions about where he had been those few weeks stalled as the community adjusted to his orders for communal effort to build up reserves. Exhausted by the physical and mental exertion in damp weather, no-one had gathered at the outdoor fireplace in days. By freeing the villagers, to all intents it appeared his plan was to settle and they were all adjusting to his newly focused leadership.

But, he couldn't resolve his internal dilemma about his intention to break his promise to Rognval. This one little ritual reminded him daily of the two promises - one which he would have to break. Indecision was preventing him from sleeping.

He called out a greeting to the seals, which had become accustomed to the strange man disturbing their morning digestions. They alone bore witness to his burden. The sea today looked choppier than the days before. Feeling calm after making his marks, Sigurd began to think about the practicalities of getting the islanders to the ceremony as autumn drew close. Distant voices drifted over the dunes, calling him to his responsibilities. Sigurd sighed.

As he turned to walk back up the path to the village, his eyes flicked up. He frowned as he thought he saw something in the sky. Looking up properly, expecting no more than a bird, he glimpsed a flash of green and lilac. His heart began to race. Sigurd grinned, then shot to the beach. Standing next to his markings, he gazed upwards once more. Hoping.

Lana watched through the thin clouds as Sigurd returned to the sand. She had only just managed to climb back up into the layer of white in time. People had emerged from the ground dwellings and were milling around. She did not dare to go lower, despite the fact that her chest fluttered wildly at the sight of him.

It was unbearable. She hovered, torn between her desperate need to be close to him, relief at seeing him, and despair at not being able to act upon her desires. It grew into a panic.

Another human was walking down the path towards the beach. And Sigurd was still watching the clouds. His beautiful face upturned, as if she had asked for it. Maybe just for her! She bit her lip and stayed true and hidden.

The intruder touched Sigurd's arm. He turned and said

something in his language to them. The other person, a tall man but greying, shook his head and laughed. Sigurd clapped the man on his back as he left again.

He waited until the other man had passed the dunes before he stripped off his top, then laid down, right on the beach. Just lying on the sand! Not a care for what he looked like or who could see him! She smiled; as before, his unpredictability enchanted her.

Lana stayed hidden, her eyes drinking in his long frame as he gazed up. Should she briefly dip down and let him know she was still here? She wasn't sure, so she rose higher to determine if the people had dispersed.

It was only then that she realised Sigurd was laid down beside some marks in the sand! Her eyes narrowed, honing in to differentiate the shapes better. She recognised the swirl - her name! Delighted, she studied the straighter lines. She couldn't recall, in her excitement, exactly what the sign meant to him. But it meant something. And, the two symbols were enclosed in a circle. She laughed as pure joy and relief flooded through her.

Her laughter drifted through the air, but not so loud that it would be heard over the dunes. Lana dipped enough to see that Sigurd was grinning. He stood, and walked down into the ripples of the tide. The seals looked around then lazily slid off their rocks, into the water and away. Sigurd carried on walking, deeper until his knees were buffeted by the sea.

He held his arms up to the sky and tilted his head back. Lana reached down, as if her arms could meet with his through the clouds. She pulled, hoping he would feel the invisible tug of her drawing out. Reaching. The tingle of his Lifeforce entered her fingertips and she drank. Pulling, harder than ever before, she breathed his essence in.

Sigurd felt the wrench. Familiar, calming and exhausting, but, irrespective of the effect he knew it would have on him, he felt comforted. She was there; she hadn't left him completely! Hope replaced the energy he understood was being drawn out of him. He had wondered about this pulled motion before, but now, this sensation of being drained was recognisably her effect.

The payoff for being around her.

And he didn't mind. He realised in that moment that he would always give freely of himself - just to have that connection with her. His wondrous Queen.

Lana watched as his knees bent and he fell further into the shallows. But she also found she couldn't stop drinking. Pulling him into herself, she knew she ought to release. But it was overwhelmingly satisfying...she wasn't sure that she could let go.

Her body reeled in the sky as it gulped in his essence, his Lifeforce. She glanced down dreamlike - the source of her joy was wavering, lurching towards the water... then falling.

The splash of cold seawater severed the ribbons. Lana descended, her eyes wide as she took in the damage to Sigurd, now face first in the water. She snapped her head around, momentarily unsure what had happened. The beach was deserted, the humans scattered through the village area, not close.

There was no-one to help him. No-one to pull him out!

She dived down through the cloud layer. Her arms were already stretched out, but she held them ready to grasp him. His chest began to float up from the depths. Hair ropes drifted around his head. Lana sped up as her hands sank down, hooking under his shoulders.

Lifting his heavy body up was only possible due to her speed of descent. Wings flapping harder to counter the extra load, she pulled. The tide was against them she realised, as Sigurd's body was buffeted by the incoming waves. She wheeled around, wings aching with the effort. He was still partially submerged, but at least his head and torso were clear of the water now.

Lana clenched her teeth together and heaved. The wave splashed over his back, splashing her feet as it met bulky resistance in its crest. She strained to pull him through the passage of the next wave, hoping it would propel them towards the beach.

She was so focused on her endeavours, she didn't notice the arms. Hands clenched around Sigurd's biceps and joined her in pulling. Looking up, her eyes flared as they recognised the tense face assisting her. Then she let go.

Disappearing upwards as fast as her wings would take her, as soon as she broke above the cloud line she stopped abruptly. Finally able to turn and look down again, her breathing laboured in and out. She watched as Issam pulled

Sigurd onto the sand. Watched as he shook him, water pouring out of his mouth.

She held her breath then, waiting for him to respond. Her mind flashed back to those terrible moments when she had last seen Sigurd so pale. When she had not known what to do, how to help him. The fear that he was taken from her - yet again - paralysed her in the sky.

Then, he coughed out, weakly. Water spat out over Issam, who looked up to the clouds. He smiled, and Lana knew that Sigurd would live. This time.

CHAPTER 31 – VOYAGE

Already pushed closer to the water's edge, the graceful lengths of the only sea-worthy boats now rested half in, half out of the surf. Wide sloped sides packed with provisions for the meal which would be needed after the ceremony. Blanket bundles stuffed under benches, and a supply of shell candles, filled with solidified seal oil and moss wicks, carefully placed in baskets. The sails rolled in readiness for hauling up and rigging lines neatly fastened.

Sigurd looked around the crowd of villagers and performed a quick head count. His men, stood to one side of the throng, were curiously silent. Anxious.

"I still think this is a stupid idea," Torv spoke up as Sigurd approached. "Why do we all have to go all the way to the other islands? Why can't they just do it here?"

Sigurd expected renewed resistance. There had been grumbling last night when he quietly informed his kinsmen that they would all be taking the villagers to perform a ritual for their faith. Talk of unfamiliar religious activies rattled the Northmen, who felt strongly that it might disrespect their gods to participate in something other than their own rites. The islanders had been unable to adequately detail what to expect, and what they had said about standing and chanting for hours in a special circle sounded very peculiar to the Northmen. He sighed, explaining his reasons once more to them all.

"You all know that we must prepare for winter here. That is what Rognval wanted. These people are not going to be sold as slaves. We need them, they need us. They say this is important for harvest preparations. We damaged their boats, so there is no other way to take them but in ours. It is time to accept we are one community now." He glared at Torv before continuing with conviction. "We are on their lands and must learn how to farm them well."

"I'm not disputing that, Yarl," Torv grumbled. "I just don't understand why we are bowing to their traditions? We own the land now, we say what happens."

"Please, Torv, let's just get in the boats. Let them do what they need to, and we can discuss this properly later?"

Torv was not an unreasonable man, and he was one of the people whom Rognval had relied upon to support him in any decisions he had made. Sigurd was uncomfortable with talking half-truths to him. Having physically recovered from his encounter with Lana, he had yet to finalise his decision on staying or leaving. Torv would be the first to ask questions and poke holes in his story. Find reasons to stay. That was partly why he hadn't even discussed his dilemma with the experienced warrior. In the meantime, he was following a delicate balancing act between the two communities.

Sigurd climbed into the shallow keel of the nearest boat. The middle cargo section at the base of the mast had been left clear for the villagers to settle into. Stepping over benches with oars laid along them, he lent out, around the huge gunwale at the front, to address them all.

"I will travel in the lead boat with Conall Finai to

navigate," he gestured towards the village elder. "Everyone else, distribute yourselves across the other boats to row, following us."

Sigurd switched language and told the islanders, "Get in the boats, we will take you to the stones now. Conall, come with me. You can guide us." Dressed in his warmest clothes now, the elder nodded, then looked over to the others in their group, smiling reassurance. A tentative trust had grown between the two leaders over the last few days.

Sigurd's saviour, the young man he found hiding by the boats called Issam, swallowed and hesitated before clambering aboard. Everyone had welcomed him into their fold, he was a hard worker as it turned out. He also seemed to subtly support the bridge that was building between the two communities. Sigurd wasn't sure where he hailed from, but the villagers appeared to know him. Even if he didn't originally come from this island, didn't live there even now, he stuck around. He kept himself to himself though, when the day's work was done, he disappeared to sleep somewhere else.

Once the majority of people were in the boats, Sigurd jumped down onto the beach again. With Torv and two others, he formed a team to push the long ships back further into the water. The Northmen crew took up the lengthy oak oars and pushed them through the holes at the rims, angling the blades down and into the sand. Villagers huddled against the sides of the boat, uncertain about the sheer size of their vessels. Not altogether trusting these invaders not to spirit them away either, despite what their giant blonde leader said and Conall's reassurance.

Pushing their shoulders into the curved hull, two a side, the Northmen pushed. Fur-lined boots scrambled to get purchase on the sand, but the smooth keel slid backwards into the water with the help of the oar shove from above. Sigurd's mouth lifted along with his heart. He was looking forward to a stretch of time on the open seas once more.

"Ho!" He called up.

"Ho!" Came back the cheerful reply from crew on Gerda - afloat and on her way. Oars descended near vertically again and pushed into the sandy shallows. There was no need for urgency, better to slide back gently. It took a few calls for the team to row in time, and Gerda gracefully became fully buoyant before slipping backwards into deeper sea. Then Rognval's flagship Bjarne followed suit.

As Sigurd pushed his boat, the Thora Brynja, he stroked her bows. He wished he had his hammer to hold as well, for luck, but it had never reappeared. As he hauled himself over the side of the ship, he felt a familiar thrill. At sea once more, to a location as yet unknown. And best of all, he had a suspicion Lana would somehow be involved. He smiled to himself as he moved forwards to the prow.

"Ho!" He shouted, and "Ho" was called.

*****

From the clear skies, Lana watched as the many boats approached the mainland. Coming from across the entire set of islands, they clustered in the ports of Rockwell, Finstown and Skaill. Mostly fishing vessels filled with passengers, the transports began to litter the beaches. A processional formed along the pathway inland. Humans would spend their midday meal time greeting one another, preparing then walking. The gathering had begun.

Lana hovered high above the village of Finstown. Issam had informed her that a village elder planned to guide the invader's vessels into berth there, on the mudflats. They would then process through the forest of Binsgarth, towards the stone circle. Lana's plan was to hide in the woods, before the ceremony, to catch just a glimpse of Sigurd. The walk to the stones would take the majority of the afternoon, so it would be a long wait. She would still have plenty of time after the procession passed to be in position above the monoliths, ready for the evening rites to start.

If he came, that is. If she could restrain herself. So much rested on this ceremony, she was convinced that she could reign in her urges if she only had sight of him. From a distance.

She watched the sea for their boats, which she knew were larger and very distinctive. The spy seemed slightly nervous about the passage, but Lana and the Captain had been firm and insisted he maintain his cover. She trusted him to remain with the villagers for the journey.

Lana could feel her wings tiring. She had been so high for so long, and running on anticipation. It had taken a vast amount of restraint to not return to Rousay and see Sigurd again. The longing, as well as the hideous perspiration and other unpleasant sensations, had returned too quickly. Only the guilt at having almost fully drained Sigurd kept her away from him. There was little else to do in Naturae it seemed, without being able to perform her usual duties. Life had been very dull. And uncomfortably crawly.

She looked at the sun, nearly full-high in the sky, and considered moving out to sea more. She couldn't risk dipping lower, from here she was as invisible as a bird. But then she saw them! A line of three ships, longer than the sailing vessels of the islanders. Wide red sails announcing their arrival as they rounded the headland. With a smile, she flew higher and whirled around, spinning. For a minute the craving which was her constant companion abated. Anticipation of satisfaction kept her heart beating fast.

When she stopped and hovered, looking down once more, her eyes widened. Seven more brightly coloured sails. on boasts as big as Sigurds' were approaching from the east! For a moment, Lana was confused. When she had seen Sigurd, she had only noticed the three boats which had landed on Rousay. Were these others from another island? Had Sigurd somehow convinced other invaders to ferry the humans to the ceremony? The seven were close together, in a formation creating two sides of a triangle. The wind was clearly with them as their progress seemed faster across the sea than Sigurd's ships.

Torn with indecision, she spun around slowly, searching the skies for the Nobles who should be joining the rite. It was too soon for them to arrive, she knew. But she hoped. She wanted answers.

No-one was there. She sighed, annoyed yet again. They

must be traveling to, or waiting at, the stone circle. As she had left so early this morning, she had no idea which, or how many, Nobles would have appeared in court. Suppressing her irritation, she flew back towards Finstown. The processional had begun its steady way up the path.

Deciding then that her original plan was best, she dived into the outskirts of the forest. She landed cross. Of all days, she now felt unprepared, uninformed. The spies would have a lot to answer for. Perhaps she shouldn't have skipped in her court duties this morning. Maybe the Nobles could have told her what was going on.

Lana flitted low through the trunks until she could hear the chatter of humans. The path through the forest was wide and edged with shrubs. The leaves were just turning red on some, still able to provide a measure of camouflage. Lana alighted near the top of a tree, set back a way from the muddy path. She made herself comfortable, crouching on a branch. A thrill went through her, tinged with fear. This was the closest she had ever been to humans, not counting Sigurd. She anticipated her dull brown dress, lacking in her usual ornate decoration, would obscure her sufficiently amongst the leaves. She hoped that before long, she would see him.

CHAPTER 32 - RED SAILS

Sigurd was one of the last to jump down into the shallows once they reached what the islanders called the Mainland. As he landed, his feet sunk into the muddy sand underneath. For a moment, he worried he might be stuck. Grabbing the side of Thora for support, his foot, with boot mercifully still on, pulled free with a squelch. He looked ahead at the others, similarly struggling to the shore, laden with bundles.

The islanders were almost at the stony part of the beach. Clumping into smaller groups, chattering to each other. He smiled, recognising excitement and anticipation. He too, was looking forward to seeing what this ritual was all about. And maybe to see Lana. Somehow.

Once he reached firmer footing, he turned briefly to look across the seas. To his horror, he saw a huge sail rounding the headland to his right. He froze, waiting. Then another.

"Torv!" He yelled, glancing backward to see if he could spot his ally. "We are not alone!"

"No," Torv called back, although he was some distance up the beach by now. "From the number of boats, looks like as many people visit here as come to Ålesund! Who knew?"

"I meant, Harold has sent more men!" As they approached, Sigurd recognised the dragon head adorning the lead boat. His heart thudded as it sank.

Torv splashed towards him, his face grave. "How did they find us?"

Sigurd shrugged. "Does it matter?"

"Maybe Ivan? When we were supposed to return?" Torv didn't sound convinced, and neither was Sigurd.

They both twisted and looked towards the dwindling numbers of people making their way up the beach. Sigurd's sense of unease turned to near panic. Looking back at the water, the boats now numbered seven. Each would contain at least forty warriors.

Whatever resistance he could drum up would be easily overwhelmed. There was little doubt in his mind about the intent of the new arrivals. Hadn't he himself been one of them not so long ago? And now, he knew what awaited the islanders. His horror grew. He had lived amongst them, knew these men by name now. Although they weren't as dear to him as his own kinsfolk, part of him had committed to living alongside them.

He turned and walked up towards the beach, his guts churning. Lana! These islanders were needed by her. A wash of prickles swept through him. To allow these people to die meant that her Queendom was somehow doomed as well.

Grabbing Torv's arm, he said urgently, "Gather our men back, quickly!"

Torv looked at him as if he were completely out of his mind. "No," he said, "You cannot mean to fight them?"

"What choice do we have?"

Torv searched his eyes and saw Sigurd's resolve. "Fighting is not always the answer, son. Even Rognval knew that. Too many of our own will be lost. Maybe Harold is here for support?"

Sigurd wavered. His experience of Harold and his men was limited. His brother had invariably said King Harold was both cruel with punishment of his Yarls and reasonable, depending on how the superstitious King's runes were interpreted at the time. By not sending back spoils, Sigurd thought it more likely Harold had decided to see for himself what had become of them. Come after his rightful share, even this late in the season.

The ships approached, oars manoeuvring them closer to where Sigurd's three vessels lay beached on the mudflats. Sigurd trudged up the shore, his hand resting on Gramr's hilt and his face grim. It would not be long before Harold's intentions were known. Sigurds mind tumbled, calculating their odds of survival and his stomach clenched.

Then, a horn blew.

Lana had waited in the tree for so long, the low vibrations of the sound jolted her out of her reverie. Absorbed in studying the faces of the humans, her growing excitement at the numbers of people who were walking towards the stone circle was tempered by a nagging frustration. She had just identified the first of what she perceived to be one of the invaders, wearing wrapped furs in the same style as Sigurd's, when the echo of a horn deafened her ears.

Glancing about, there seemed no immediate source. But the noise was alien to her, and the humans on the path. They looked around also in bewilderment. In fear. The entire line of people stopped, a ripple of uncertainty startling them to attention. Belongings dropped to the ground. Some of the men reached for bows slung across their backs.

Lana dared not move, frozen in a crouch. Now that they were alerted, a mass of arrows could be unleashed if she gave away her location. The woods fell silent. Lana tried to breathe normally, but her heart was racing. She was trapped.

Sigurd picked up his pace as he reached firmer ground, calling for his men. The horn from the approaching boats confused him. If they intended to fight, why announce their presence further? Was it a hail for attention? His attention? Or a rallying call? He was too far away to hear if the warriors in the boats had begun the prayers. But he still anticipated that before long, the sound of beating weapons banging against shields would begin drumming up the fighting urge.

Even if he could avoid a fight, he needed a show of numbers behind him. A few of his men stopped and turned towards him. More appeared - emerging from the pathway between the houses closest to the beach, alerted to trouble. Sigurd paused and unsheathed Gramr. More weapons were pulled out as his kin wordlessly understood the extent of the problem lying ahead of them in the shallows.

Hearing Torv's heavy breath behind him, Sigurd turned. "We need firmer ground."

Panting, Torv nodded and carried on running. The group gathered at the top of the beach where the land shifted from sand to soil. They clustered around Sigurd, focused on what his plan would be.

Sigurd glanced over their shoulders. The path beyond held a few of the men from the village who had followed the Northmen back. Their faces spoke of the fear - they had already been through this before. Sigurd raised the arm not holding Gramr, beckoning them to join as well. But they stayed in the shadows, still not trusting the new leader. At least they had bows, Sigurd thought. There was a chance that some of the islanders could escape and still eek out an existence.

Sigurd turned to his brothers-in-arms, "It's Harold," he confirmed. They muttered curses and grumbled, but he gave them his options. "We either stand and fight for what is ours, or we accede and hope they leave."

Torv immediately butted in, "It's a losing battle, Yarl." Sigurd turned and glared. He could see some of his men agreed.

"We don't have to fight, I know. But we claimed these lands in Rognval's name. Do you want to give it straight to Harold?"

The choice before the Northmen was not straightforward. Discovery of new lands meant they owed allegiance primarily to the Yarl who landed on them, depending on if the voyage had been sanctioned or not by their local King. They were their own men there though, removed from the dictates of the King back home. They would not need to 'gift' an amount of their profits to him as well as Sigurd. In time, perhaps Sigurd would call himself King also, create other Yarls to manage the territories.

Or, they could 'welcome' the newcomers, and try to say it was claimed already for Harold. Rognval had sailed in this direction with Harold's blessing, but the instruction hadn't been to settle. Just explore and take what they could. Although they would have some explaining to do, they might live long enough to stay if the islands were offered up as territory for the king.

But, the islanders would almost certainly die or be taken as slaves. Their houses ransacked for treasure and left burning. Sigurd knew that this strike had come at the worst of times as, if he understood the elders correctly, the entire population of the local islands would be gathered in this one place.

Time was short. It was late summer and there was only a small, but sufficient, voyage window in which to return to their homelands before winter set in. Harold was not here to waste time talking. The opportunity to leisurely deliberate ownership of these lands had been missed.

And now he was here. Sigurd could hear the throb of swords beating the metal rims of many shields.

Tentatively the humans in the woods turned, looking towards the small township not far behind them. Their paralysis was lifting, and panic setting in. Lana looked down the pathway and saw the tail end of the line had disappeared. Women began to drag children through the trees and off the track. Bravely, the men stood watch, bows raised and brandishing sticks. Crouching on the branch, Lana briefly considered sliding down to join them. Fear emanated from the humans - to her, it appeared as tiny wavering slivers of grey. Not attractive, but curious. The taste of it perplexed her and the memory of her mother returning from battle during the Sation wars rose into her mind.

She heard a rustle at the base of her tree, and peered down through the leaves. Below her, in the undergrowth, stood Issam. She hissed his name quietly.

The spy looked up. His eyes widened as he recognised her high up in the branches. She smelled his fright - the familiarity of fae emotions soothed and emboldened her. Issam's natural inclination to blend in had prompted him to conceal himself, she wasn't sure if he had unconsciously found her tree or whether it was merely chance.

The human women were trying to hide themselves, shushing noisy children as they pulled bracken over crouched bodies. Lana watched as the men silently gestured to each other to return to the town. As they left, the forest once again fell quiet.

Lana waited, watching until the bows and their owners moved out of sight, before moving. With a last glance at the nearby vegetation, checking no humans were close by, she lent into her wings and fluttered down.

As she landed, she pulled on Issam's arm and they crouched. Hiding behind the trunk of the tree, Lana's dark eyes met his. "We need to find him," she whispered. Issam shook his head quickly, his lips squeezed together.

"Where is he?" Lana pressed.

Issam jabbed his finger back in the direction of the settlement.

"Give me your cloak."

With shaking hands, Issam unclasped the wooden toggle and pulled it off himself. The rough wool warmed Lana as she shuffled it over her back and dropped her wings so they laid flatter. Then, staying low, she crept towards the track. As she reached the tree tunnel, she flicked the cloak between her wings and flew straight up.

CHAPTER 33 – TO THE DEATH

Sigurd faced the beach, Gramr planted in front of him and rested his hands on the hilt. "You must decide now, each of you. But one way or another, this land is ours. If we live here, we can die here."

Behind him, he could hear the shuffling of boots and swords being pulled. His warriors fanned out around him. He looked down the sides of the line, nodding. "And so we stand." He was gratified to see that all of them had decided to stay with him, hold their ground.

Before them, the boats had beached. Sigurd swallowed as he absorbed the numbers which then began jumping down. He gripped Gramr's hilt, but kept her poised upright between his splayed legs. Waiting to see what Harold would do.

The army calmed their battle chants as they splashed their way through the shallows and then reached the sludgy mud. Progress up the beach was comically uneven as stomping feet sank. Warriors wobbled for balance as they tried to pull fur-lined boots up and out of the boggy waters. Sigurd tried not to smirk, as he felt a measure of relief that Rognval hadn't invaded this particular land. Their entire surprise attack would have been sunk had they attempted.

Mud did not deter Harold's men, however. They gathered in a semicircle, paused by some unheard command not to advance until the King himself was present. A rotund figure emerged from the middle of the row. His face was obscured by a helmet with a long nose guard, shining in the sunlight. By his side walked his fabled see'r, an old man revered by many and trusted with the onerous task of for-telling. Harold did not need to wear a crown to demonstrate his position, the huge dragon head on the lead boat had already announced him.

He raised his sword, aiming up the beach towards them. Sigurd's heart thumped to the point of painful. The warriors let out a cry and began to beat their hilts to their shields. But they didn't advance.

Sigurd stepped forwards, Gramr now held by his leg. He walked with his head held high, staring directly at Harold and doing his best ignore glancing down the lines of warriors. Midway down the beach yet still on the firmer sand, he stopped. The distance between them still gave his men enough time to retreat if necessary, but he was close enough for a shouted conversation.

"We claimed these lands in the name of Yarl Rognval the Fearless. I am Yarl now."

Harold tilted his head, "You?" He laughed. The crowd behind him joined in, recognising the misfit brother of the respected former Yarl.

Sigurd waited until the noise died down. Torv appeared by his side. Glancing to his sides, Sigurd realised that the other men had also moved down, off the solid ground. He tried not to think about that strategic error. They were side by side with him. That was what mattered.

"If you have come for treasure," Sigurd said, "there is none." He gestured behind, "No churches, no gold."

"Then why did you bother?" Harold laughed.

Sigurd didn't answer.

"Where is Rognval?" Harold asked.

"In Valhalla, Lord King," replied Sigurd, thrusting his chin out.

Harold leaned forward slightly, "You? Defeated Rognval and claimed Yarl?" He shook his head, "I would never have believed it."

"Rognval fell during a raid," Sigurd explained. "He bestowed the lands to me before passing."

"Did he die well?" Harold said, almost conversationally.

"He died with honour." Sigurd saw an opportunity. "But, the people here are not without skill. Or protection."

Harold's chin jutted back. "With what army? I see no army here? Except mine." He grinned cruelly, the backdrop of men behind him barely restraining their laughter.

Sigurd thought back to Naturae, the winged warriors he had seen training.

"There are creatures which serve these lands. Fearsome. From other worlds."

"What are you doing?" Torv hissed at him.

"The shores of the Guds are close by - they claimed Rognval as payment for his presence."

Sigurd was improvising wildly now, but he had Harold's attention.

"We now protect these lands to honour his sacrifice. I do not advise you continue, Lord King. These are not lands which you should try to take for yourself. You would not want to suffer the same fate as Rognval."

Harold looked around his men. His lips pursed. That a respected Yarl had fallen to strange creatures was not what he had anticipated discovering when he arrived here.

Torv hissed under his breath again at Sigurd. "Why are you saying these lies, brother?"

"Because it's not lies, friend."

Torv raised his eyebrow and met Sigurd's eyes. They glanced over at Harold then back at each other. "Then where is this mysterious army?" Torv muttered.

The long-haired see'r whispered something in the King's ear. Then everyone watched as he crouched down next to Harold's feet and threw some bones on the sand. The men behind craned to get a look, and for a moment, a collective breath held.

The elder looked up at his King and Harold decided who he believed more.

With an almighty roar, he lifted his blade. His army began to rush up the beach, shields, spears and blades in front of them.

Sigurd dropped his weight onto his heels and prepared for the blows. Shieldless, his men at least had swords and determination. He pulled his shorter seax blade out from his belt, holding it in his left hand ready to stab. More like a knife, the slim bone handle was warm from being close to his skin.

From behind them, arrows rained down, hitting the sand at the feet of Harold's army. The charge didn't pause. Sigurd and his men remained tensed, watching the feet of the army slip in the looser surface.

Another release of arrows found more targets as the hordes ran up the slight incline towards the settlement. A few bodies dropped to the ground, others carried on with slim sticks jutting out from their limbs as if they were no more than arm decoration. Sigurd was grateful for the villagers' intervention, but that didn't prevent the sinking feeling that it was a futile gesture.

With a clash of swords, Sigurd pushed Gramr down and plunged his seax deep into the chest of the first warrior to attack him. Wheeling round, Gramr then slashed the thighs of the next. The third to rush him used his shield to push Gramr out of the way, but Sigurd had been expecting it. The blow glanced off his rib cage as he spun away, bringing up the seax to deliver a fatal wound to the back.

With a burst of energy, Sigurd swung and stabbed, kicked and wheeled. The attackers kept advancing, pushing the fight further up the beach and into the settlement. Their sheer numbers forcing Sigurd's men to move back, just to get space to dance the deadly duels.

Sigurd glanced over, Torv was holding his own close by. Spittle dangled from his mouth but his concentration was fierce and he was giving the fighter in front of him everything that decades of experience taught. As the next warrior prepared to charge at Sigurd, he was stopped by an arrow to the eye. He fell forwards to Sigurd's feet, dead before he hit the stones.

With no-one immediately in front of him now, Sigurd

wheeled around, his eyes frantically scanning for the helpful assassin. There, standing on the rooftops, were familiar islanders. They were picking off the invaders as best they could, faces screwed up in determination as they took careful aim. Sigurd knew it wouldn't be long before the army overwhelmed their brief resistance and came for the natives as well.

He had to warn them, tell them to get away before it was too late. "Go!" he shouted in their language. "Go into the land. Hide!"

He jogged to the dwellings, the noise of the battle too loud for an individual cry to be heard. Sigurd hoped this landmass was large enough for them to be able to escape, start a new life elsewhere. "Go to other boats, other villages!"

The desperate tone in his voice reached the man closest to him. He dropped his bow and stared. Sigurd ran closer, calling up to the archers to get down, run. He paused, partly to catch his breath, and leaned against a wall to watch the islanders scrabbling down the roofs.

From behind, Sigurd felt a blade slash across his legs. His tendons severed, he screamed. As he staggered forward, he blinked wildly in confusion. The ground rushed up at him.

He collapsed, turning his torso as he fell so he could see the eyes of his assailant. If there was any justice to be had, should be Harold, he thought. But it wasn't, such was the wheel of fate. Just some dumb, unknown warrior who then raised his arms high, bringing down Sigurd's doom with one glinting swoop.

Lana felt the stab to her heart just as cleanly as the blade swiped Sigurd. From the skies, she had watched the entire battle, not able to intervene at all. At first, when the fighting began, she felt such pride. Not only had her love tried to warn off the man in the helmet, but when that failed, he had stood his ground and decided to protect the humans.

Her heart was in her mouth as she admired him fight. Sigurd moved with a grace which belied his human form, balletic as a master fae soldier. She had been utterly convinced he would somehow defeat any attacker.

But then, her thrill turned to horror. Why had he gone back into the settlement? She thought she heard him trying to tell the islanders to go, but the noise of the battle below on the beach was distracting. She couldn't hear clearly yet couldn't get closer. Then, she watched as he fell. And did not get up.

Without thinking about the consequence, she dived down behind the cluster of houses. Landing, running, she didn't care who saw her. Her feet barely registered the chill of the stones as she raced towards him.

The blood was beginning to pool out of him. She glanced around. His killer had moved on. The archers were clambering down thatched roofs and fleeing into the woods. Down on the beach, she could hear the cries of the ongoing battle, the clang and thuds of bodies crashing together.

And there was her dear Sigurd. She put her hands out to turn his head towards her. As she did so, a bubble of blood pushed out of his mouth, and his eyes flicked to meet hers. Lana caught her breath - the smell of his blood attacking her senses. She breathed out, gazing at him as if that would push the sudden temptation away. Then, as his eyelids twitched, she registered that he was nevertheless hanging on, his Lifeforce still present.

She panicked, that same feeling of dread she had before when she held him in Naturae spread over her. But this was different, there would be no cure for a hole that size in his chest. No stopping the bleeding from his ankles.

There was no choice, but she couldn't let him die here. Like this. It had to be on her terms. Lana lent in closer and whispered, "I'm sorry."

She drew back and his eyes met hers - filling with tears of regret. He blinked acquiescence and tried to smile as she inhaled. Just a little, just enough.

His Lifeforce immediately flowed through her, the ribbon she pulled seemed to ease him as well. With his vitality coursing through her, she looped her arms under his shoulders. His face fell into her neck as she lifted him up. Enormous wings unfurled behind her. Smoothly she rose up, into the sky. Away.

CHAPTER 34 - VINEALLY

An unprompted and vague memory of her mother telling the tale of her pupation appeared to Lana as she tried to distract herself from the pain in her arms, carrying Sigurd home. She had said, 'Nothing compares to the torment and love that a Royal is borne from.' At the time, just a young pupae, she had thought her mother referred to the stringent rules she lived under. The harsh lessons about ruling which being Queen would expose her to. But now, broken by this agony of lost love, she wondered if it might have meant something more.

Lana didn't think she could have gone much further when the welcome shimmer of mist beckoned. Turning her back on the violent streaks of sunset, her mind resolved. Sigurd's dead weight, cradled in her arms, was still warm as she set down on the Pupaetory balcony. Then she kicked open the doors and dragged him through. The space inside was sufficient for her to resume flying but, having stopped for a moment to deal with the doors, her path through the air now felt lumbering and awkward.

At the end of the long chamber, the far door to the vines was propped ajar. Panting with exertion, Lana dipped down and slowed to bring herself and her lover through the low aperture. She looked around, quickly assessing which vine was in the best of health.

Then she saw it, right at the back. A shoot which had somehow taken root but not yet been cultivated. Pale yellow, its leaves were just unfurling. Were this any other time, she might have ripped it out to make room for stronger, healthier vines to flourish. But this vine grew in the corner of the bed, where it was dark and comforting. She felt in her heart that this was the right plant - grown anew from indistinguishable parentage. Fresh, therefore unbound to a specific destiny, but it was weak and undernourished.

She pulled Sigurd closer and then moved her hand to his head as she lowered herself and his body down. Her fingers splayed to take the weight of his skull, gently bringing it to the ground so she could see him once more. His pale face etched itself in her mind as she gazed down on it.

His blue eyes moved slowly to hers, rousing as he realised they had stopped moving. But the blood kept weakly pushing out of him, soaking into the earth. Lana tried to bring ribbons out of herself, to bless into him, but there were none to be had. She didn't dare take the last strand of Lifeforce she felt within him.

His hand reached up and stroked her hair. She clutched it - not wanting him to waste his last moments, touching her. She didn't deserve it. She had failed. She couldn't save him. "Why?" She whispered under her breath, more to herself than to him. Why could she not change this? Why had this happened to her?

His lips moved, whispering. "No hammer... Thor's hammer."

Lana frowned, confused. Sigurd seemed to understand and

tried with his last breaths to clarify.

"Hammer lost, Sigurd lost."

"What hammer?" Lana said desperately.

"The man who hurt... took."

His eyes rolled backwards. Only a thin white sliver of the once vivid blue eyes remained. Lana could feel he was leaving her. She could barely sense his Lifeforce. She shook his head and his eyes slowly came back to meet hers, but they were glazed over, not focussing on her. Not reacting to her at all.

Lana's lip began to wobble as the enormity of what was about to happen to him hit her. This was beyond her control. She could do nothing to prevent his passing. Between them, the fizzle in their gaze dwindled. She laid her head down on his heart, clutching him close. The beat of him slowed. Then stopped.

Lana waited there, hoping against hope to hear another thump. For something to happen to him. With her mother, at the instant of death, her being had changed and her body became ethereal. Lana couldn't release her arms from Sigurd. Afraid that he too would disappear.

She sat motionless for hours, tears seeping out of her, and his blood dripping out of him. She was so utterly alone, so completely drained, that it didn't occur to her to look at him again until the darkness turned to dawn.

The change in light brought with it a quiet crackling sound. At first, only a tiny whisper of a noise, then a whoosh of a leaf moving against another as it vied for the sunshine streaming in through the windows. Lana raised her head.

The vine in the corner had grown. Overnight, the yellowed leaves had opened, greened. Underneath the largest hung two cocoons. Lana sat up. She laid Sigurd's cold head down on the ground carefully. She caressed his firm chin and bent over to kiss his stiff lips. Then, she leaned towards the stem and examined the leaf-enclosed buds. With gentle fingers, she stroked one of them. The smooth outer layer was warm!

She gasped and curled her fingertips around the cocoon. It was full, healthy. Growing.

Lana's face broke into a smile. Had she done it? Had she and Sigurd somehow managed to create a royal? Possibly two? She looked down at Sigurd. "You are a father," she whispered. Her voice sounded wobbly, strange even to her.

Standing now, she pulled him away from the base of the vine and began to dig. Using her hands, ignoring the tears which dripped from her jaw, she scooped aside the soil until a shallow depression circled the stem. She pushed Sigurd, almost rigid and heavy, into position. Then, shaking with the finality of it, she covered her lover with soft earth.

Finally, she sat back on her heels and studied the vine. The impact of Sigurd's death hit her. The raised lumps of his body curling around the earth, which a moment ago previously had seemed like a suitable place for him to be, now looked like a wall, coiling protectively around their precious offspring.

Her eyes filled as she thought about the last wall she had torn down. She had tried so hard to save him then. And for what? It had been in vain. She had opened her soul to the feelings he evoked within her. Only for him to leave her, as her mother had. Leave her alone. Now there was just this void of grief, a deep chasm of pain filling her up.

Lana wheeled around and strode out of the Vine Room. Her fists clenched and she allowed herself to feel the anger rising. Her wings stretched outwards, engulfing her heart with fire. As she reached the double doors, her ire was incandescent. Dark and red like the blood covering her skirt.

The bright sky overhead offered no relief from the swathes of self-loathing coursing through her. "No more," she screamed at it. Even as she took off, flying faster and faster upwards, the pain did not relent.

"No. More."

The scream dissipated into the winds. She wheeled around. The noise had gone, but her anger hadn't. She dived down maybe the jolt of a hard landing would jolt this horror away from her.

It didn't.

She stomped over to the huge twin trees which had seemed to mean so much to Sigurd. She stood underneath, gazing up at the tangle of branches overhead. The leaves which remained on the ash tree had decayed into a violent purple-red colour, just about to fall. Between the leafy canopy, the sunlight poked through. The impression it left in her eyes as she blinked and turned away outlined a shape. A contour that was familiar to her, but had been absent of late on Sigurd. A hammer shape. She knew at once what Sigurd had been talking about - the necklace he wore!

She rushed back to the clearing. The dark tunnels of the Beneath beckoned her. Offering comfort from the invasive brightness of the sunshine. She marched towards it, snarling. Inside, the narrow passages barely registered as she stomped downward. Deep within the belly of the earth, the cool air caused the hairs on her bare arms to stand on end. She became aware of the crawling sensation beginning again, tickling its insipid destruction underneath her skin. The yearning began, but fed into her fury.

She passed two guards lurking, jumping to attention as they saw her approach. Stomping past them, she snapped, "Where is Tolant kept?"

One of them scurried ahead of her, drawing out a key. He hovered in the small space before a doorway, then beat a hasty retreat into the tunnels having unlocked it. Lana pursed her lips, gritting her teeth together so hard. She kicked the door in and there he was.

Tolant had heard her angry approach and was on his feet, at the far end of the cell. She glared at him through the darkness in silence. Her breaths heavy. Fists clenched.

Tolant reached out a hand, "Your Highness?" His voice sounded wispy in the earth hole.

Lana could barely speak. For a moment she questioned why she had even come to him. Then she remembered. His fault. His fault Sigurd died.

"Where is the hammer you took?" Her voice was chilling as it cut through the darkness.

Tolant shook his head.

Lana flew at him. Her hands unclenched into claws which pinned him to the earth walls behind. She narrowed her eyes. "Once more, where is his hammer?"

Tolant gazed up at her, his lips whimpering.

"I didn't know!" he said.

"Even now, you lie to me!" Lana snarled. She shook him against the wall. It was unsubtle as a torture method, she recognized, but did not have the patience for his kind of painful information extraction.

Tolant dropped his head. She just knew that when she brought it back up he would have that thin sneer on it. She was right.

"Has he survived still? Even though I took his power?" Tolant's snide words cut her afresh.

"Where is it?" Lana screeched, her face pressed close to his.

"A Queen such as yourself has no need of toys, trinkets and tokens," Tolant spat out. "You ought to be grateful that I tried to preserve the order which the daemon threatened."

"You did nothing but betray me. You are nothing!"

Tolant glared at her, defiant to the last. "I am what you made me, your Highness. I have evidence that everything I have done has been in your name. To protect and serve only you. Proof displayed for all to see is in my rooms. Without his power tokens, he should have been nobody to you."

He stared at her, then raised an eyebrow. "You didn't make him bleed did you?"

The rage rose too far within Lana. Now that she had her answer, there was no holding it in any more. She drew her head away from his and watched the fear enter his eyes as her lips stretched back.

Lana leaned into his neck and pierced it, not caring that

this was breaking the cardinal rule of sanctity of all fae life. She drank deeply, absorbing his knowledge, his essence. All the darkness that manipulated him. The pride which he had in his rise to her side, partaking of her power. Her eyes flared. Never before had she tasted such emotion from a creature. Not even humans held their lifetimes captive within in such a way. She was the one Queen. She could take whatever she wanted.

Her mouth dripped with his blood, but she pulled on still. Underneath her fingertips, she felt his skin shrivel. Ragged and dirty robes fell lank to the floor, slipping off his body as it retracted into itself. Finally, she dragged herself from him. Tilting her head back, a scream of rage absorbed into the surrounding earth. Dropping the carcass, she hovered in the middle of the cell, the noise pouring out of her. Her body vibrated with raw anguish and anger.

CHAPTER 35 – HAMMER

Some years later, on the day of Pupaetion, a deep frost clung to the branches. Tiny glinting ice stars heralded a purity and hope which was deceptive. Lana was not present when the cocoons split. She missed their first laboured cries. Strong and healthy sounds from perfectly formed twin mouths. The Pupaetory nurses fluttered about the new arrivals with excitement. These two cocoons were the last left in the Pupaetory. No more had been created since - what the workers had taken to calling the recent times - the 'Great Sadness' had begun.

When the Head Pupaetory Nurse scurried into her chambers with the news, Lana gazed at her, incredulity spreading across her face. The miracle of their existence - and their continued development - too unbelievable to accept without proof. The Nurse's greying hair quivered as she adamantly assured that the pupae were healthy and wanted to meet her. As if pupae could talk, Lana snorted to herself. Regardless, now with a leaden heart, she knew she would have to visit the Pupaetory, just the once more, to view the evidence of her undoing.

Since Sigurd's death, Lana had cloistered herself in her chambers. The workers serving her tiptoeing in and out with a succession of animals, or latterly, fish. They snuck glances at her whilst they cleaned, wondering what she was doing with the scrolls on her desk.

In her absence, the Council had met and decreed that the running of Naturae should continue with her nominally in place. Their collective opinion, which was disseminated via the Captain to all worker fae, was that the Queen needed to rest in between ceremonies. Her mannerisms, verging now on the extreme, were to be cosseted. Quietly endured until such a time as she recovered sufficiently to resume her duties.

The growth of the twin cocoons, despite not being blessed by the Queen, was the subject of much speculation. The Council very much hoped that the new Royal pupae would be female and thus prevent the Queendom from having to be passed into the care of an alternative Royal. Naturae had been ruled over by this family for more centuries than the elders could count. The few remaining elder Nobles of the dominion were sceptical of interference from abroad. The news of not one, but two Royal cocoons growing - somehow - out of the devastation, was welcome. The Council's relief at probable succession was palpable during their conventions following the failed autumn ceremony.

To await this glorious Pupation day, and whilst the Queen 'recovered' sufficiently, the Nobles remained in Naturae. This was, in part, because sustenance could still be found here. Forest animals hunted and presented by the workers kept everyone's needs sated. The invaders had now ravaged their own territories. The original islanders taken or killed. Ceremonial gatherings had dwindled until there were only a handful of desperate people, scavenging out an existence.

Within a remarkably short space of time, for faekind, all vestiges of the rituals of life would be forgotten by the remaining humans.

Despite the news that she was a mother again, Lana's body hung dull with tiredness. She dismissed the nurse without thanks and stood to face the mirror. Her hair, once lustrous, hung lank around her shoulders. Red-rimmed eyes seemed enormous in her thin, pale face. Peaceful rest continued to elude her. Nights were filled with agonising dreams only interrupted by heart-racing sweats as she jolted awake.

She never spoke of these sensations, not to anyone. Over time, she became more and more convinced that were she to even speak of it, then the entire anguish would come pouring out of her. And who could she unburden herself to? There was no-one left, no-one she trusted at all.

Scribbled notes detailing her anger, her longing, and her loss, built a defence around her, hiding inside the betrayal she felt, the failure and the grief. Never again would anybody dismantle it. At the end of each day, as night fell, she burned the scrolls. Red flames hid her shame and kept her secrets. The scrawled words disintegrated into ashes, which a worker would rake out and dispose of each morning.

Instead, today, she cloaked her wall in the finest of dresses. Piled her hair up, fastened into a crown that would remain on her head alone. She looked once again in the mirror, assessing the dignified figure which stared back. There was just one thing missing.

Lana crossed to her pillow and reached underneath.

Wrapping her fingers around the leather thong, she kissed the silver hammer in her palm. Then, still clutching the token, she walked out of her chamber for the first time in years, chin held high.

She flew slowly down the hallways, lined with hopeful faces. Her dark green wings propelled her gracefully over the balconies and in through the doors of the Pupaetory.

As she landed, her face hardened, and she held her breath. Her lips clenched together to the point of painful as she steeled herself to look at her successors. How strange, she thought, to meet who would rule on after one's death. To know that they would be your replacement. It didn't carry the comfort it should.

The pupae lay swaddled in two carved cots. Some fae had gone to the trouble of inlaying silver swirls to the heads of the dark wood. Even the sheen of the delicate cloth the twins were wrapped in hinted at the special nature of the youngsters. Lana peered into the small receptacles, her hands clutching at her skirt.

The first was clearly a male, his fine features edged with a strong but narrow chin. A mop of ash-coloured hair fought to escape the wrappings. The pupae's eyes were open, and the deep brown of her own gazed vacantly out, disturbed by the change from light to shadow. Lana frowned. A boy could not be Queen. The Nurse had failed to mention this to her.

She gritted her teeth together, for once pushing down the immediate rage which sprang up at this abject failure to disclose something so important. With a single pace, she strode over to the other cot and glanced down, fully expecting to see a similar pupae resting there.

However, bright blue eyes fixated on her immediately. Lana's mouth dropped open. A chill ran down her spine and she froze, unable to move closer. Framing those unmistakably familiar eyes was a shock of bright golden hair, waving with a slight curl around the most precious of faces. Lana's heart almost melted as she gazed over its soft skin.

"A girl?" She croaked out, as the pain of her loss washed over her once again.

"Yes, your Highness," the Head Nurse replied softly.

"She is...formed?"

"Perfectly."

Lana breathed out.

"She is so beautiful," the Nurse ventured. "Do you have names for them?"

Lana thought for a moment. "Aioffe. Call her what she is. Beautiful. Radiant. Also, the beginning. You can tell her that. She is the beginning of hope."

A ripple spread through the assembled fae, and they began to murmur amongst themselves.

The Head Nurse asked tentatively, "Would you like to hold them?"

Lana turned away from expectant faces, tightening her fingers around the hammer clenched in her palm. The familiar nobbles of its shape painfully pushed deep into her bones. Any child of his would only be a reminder of what she had lost. Of the pain she now lived with daily. Lana thought back to the noisy human boy at the stone circle - his need for his parents' attention. A child, even if it was royal, was too chaotic for her to bear opening her heart to. The risk was too great.

No, these children must be raised the same as any other worker fae. Perhaps some small exception for the girl, her own quarters maybe. In time, she would instruct the nurses in how to prepare her for royal duties, but there was no hurry on that. Many centuries would pass before it was even likely to be needed, if ever.

The Queen sighed, her mind resolved. The fragile future of Naturae depended on her alone, and she could not allow any more upset to threaten it. That was her duty, as it would be the duty of her daughter, eventually.

She then made a decision which placed the final stone in her Queen's wall. Holding the pupae served no purpose.

Flapping her wings and rising from the path, the nurse noticed their vivid green momentarily seemed to blacken.

"No," Lana said. "No," she whispered to herself as her heart thumped in response. She focused her eyes on the doors and blinked away the light. Her ribs tightened briefly, then accepted the absolute darkness enveloping her soul.

She flew away from hope, and love, and risking the destiny of Naturae. Lana, Queen of Naturae, would rule alone.

In the corner of the Pupaetory, a leaf fell from the vine which had so recently held the royal cocoons. Aioffe let out a loud cry from her cradle, and the nurse took her little wrinkled hand and tightened her lips.

"Aioffe," she whispered, the babe's blue eyes gazing up at her in response to her voice. "There is hope in every child. I fear we shall need it more than ever before."

HISTORICAL NOTE

In this story, I liberally interpreted the somewhat contradictory historical accounts from the Norse sagas which describe the Viking invasion of the Orkney islands. That said, some of my Northmen characters are based on real people. Rognvald Eysteinsson was the first Yarl of Orkney, a position given to him by King Harold, then handed down to his brother Sigurd. For plot purposes, I have glossed over Rognvald's subsequent invasions into Scotland in the late 800's.

Through my research, I have come to realise that our perception of the Vikings is largely tainted by their portrayal as violent marauders. Indeed, I imagine that were I to be faced with terrifyingly large men wielding weapons arriving on huge boats, I would form a negative impression of them too! However, there is no denying their influence on British culture, and indeed their bravery and reach in global exploration.

Dear Reader

If you have enjoyed this book, why not visit www.escapeintoatale.com to find out more about Jan Foster and the Naturae Book series?

A Polite Request:

I am an independently published author and as such, reviews are critical to successfully getting my stories seen by readers. It would mean the world to me if you could leave a review on Amazon or Goodreads about this book so that others can find it!

The first two chapters of Book 1 of the Naturae Series - **Disrupting Destiny** - follows overleaf, I hope you enjoy them!

Order your copy now!
https://www.books2read.com/disruptingdestiny

Available April 2021

Book 2 of the Naturae Series, **Anarchic Destiny**

King Henry VIII has died, and chaos will follow. It is the ideal moment for daemons to weave their ideas into the future of England. Suspicion and creativity battle face to face in this deadly fight for acceptance.

Available Autumn 2021

THE NATURAE SERIES
DISRUPTING DESTINY

Hunted and in hiding for a century, two outcast Fae soulmates have their dreams of freedom and eternal life together ripped apart after a violent confrontation with a ruthless figure from the past.

Racing against time itself forces Annabella to choose - confront or flee from her destiny. The shadowy world she knew before haunts her but, battling heartache believing her lover is dead, can she find the strength to be the change Naturae needs now? Rebellion looms but to avert it she must challenge history, as well as accept a solitary future.

Once a mortal, homebody Joshua must desperately navigate the turbulence of Reformation England in a quest to recover his love, whilst finally reconciling his faith with his unnatural state. Traversing North East England and Scotland trying to find her mystical kingdom, he just has to survive long enough to save her…

The fate of an entire race rests on their shoulders, but can destiny be changed? Rebellion, danger and intrigue threaten the future in a thrilling journey, weaving Tudor times with magical fantasy.

Disrupting Destiny – forever isn't certain, trust no-one…

CHAPTER 1 – DISRUPTING DESTINY

1427AD - South West England

The growing pains were excruciating. Tearing his skin, continually stretching as new cells formed, split and formed again. In his conscious moments his body railed against the constraints of the cocoon, ripples of agony searing through his long limbs, straining for release yet finding none. He had no concept of how long he had endured the pain, only that it was ever-present, peaking until he could bear it no more.

Gradually, he became more lucid as the pain diminished. In these brief moments, he was aware of light filtering through the thin membrane, and a shadow hovering over it. This time, consciousness arrived to the realisation that the agony had gone. His nails unclenched from his palms, leaving bloody half-moons. Working his hands up past his naked chest to his face, his fingers sought instinctively to remove the source of the suffocation. The shadow darkened, and he heard it say a muffled, "My love..."

The yearning to join the voice, to be free, drove his panic. A guttural sound came from his throat as he clawed frantically at the suffocating veil. With a squelch, his nails snagged a hole and he pulled, straining with his entire being to enlarge it. Taking a huge gasp of breath, he realised that tender hands were smoothing limp membrane away from his face.

"Open your eyes," she said, that gentle yet somehow familiar voice again, as her touch wiped mucus from his nostrils. The panic subsided in him and, for a moment, he was aware only of his heart thumping uncomfortably in his chest, beginning to slow as the breaths came easier. He opened his eyes and raised his head towards the direction of the voice. They blurred before clearing, then began blinking in the light streaming through the window behind the shape.

Part of him expected the pain to return when he moved his limbs, yet instead the joints felt lubricated, smooth. Stretching out, he became aware again of the cool, wet membrane, now slipping from his naked body. Feeling it with his toes and hands, it suddenly revolted him. He instinctively jerked away from it, falling towards her.

His knee hit the earthen floor hard as he fell, and the jolt sent a quick wave of pain through his leg. To his surprise, it wasn't the same kind of agony as he had so recently endured - quite dull by comparison. A pale hand clasped his arm, supporting him as he straightened to look up at her properly.

"My love..." she repeated, his eyes finally came into focus on her mouth. Small, white teeth peeked through smiling red lips, framed by long white-blonde hair. He knew her...he knew that voice and he knew her smell. Lavender, witch hazel and fir - all mingled together to provide a scent that was uniquely hers. His arm reached up to touch her face, still not daring to speak, and in one smooth movement, he stood to his full height to be nearer to her. As he breathed in, her arms joined his and they clasped each other. Their eyes locked together, searching for confirmation that their very souls were still intact.

From the edge of his vision, he glimpsed iridescent wings unfurling from behind her. Mesmerised, the light from the window aperture shone through them like stained glass, illuminated and shimmering. He felt his shoulder blades quiver and, turning his head, saw his own newly formed wings rise up, silvery translucent grey yet with the radiance of hers catching the sunshine. In wonder, she reached out and stroked his wings edges; it tickled like rain falling on cold skin.

His senses exploded at her touch and the immediate surroundings rushed at him, overwhelming him. He felt the vibrations of the worms wriggling through the earth beneath his bare feet. A distant call of a lone seagull flying high above, circling for a fish to dive for. The rustling of the fir trees in the breeze accompanied by a crackle of pine cones opening to share their seed. Burnt ashes, chalky and spent as they lay in the hearth. The air too tasted sour with a tinge of iron lingering on its edges. He swallowed to clear the taste from his throat, hoping the other smells and sounds would fade as well.

The blood. He remembered the blood. Mingling warm and salty, rich, red. He had tasted the long history of her Lifeforce, and she his - a much shorter, human life.

He recalled he'd needed something - anything - to take the pain from the injury away. And he would have done whatever it took to stay with her. Her blood held the only promise she could make him at the time, and neither of them had understood the consequences. Until now.

Then, the change had begun. Numbing his senses as she bundled him tightly, suffocatingly. Somehow she must have known he needed to be wrapped - she hadn't mentioned it before he was sure. He looked at her in horror, reeling from the invasion of the memory. Stepping back, his face formed the question before he could speak it.

"I didn't know...." she tailed off, reaching once more for him. "I...I'm sorry. I'm sorry for the pain. I've never done this before," she explained. "The wings are....unexpected. I thought it would be like the animals, you'd just heal. But then you were in so much pain, I felt I needed to cocoon you, like a pupae. To make it easier to change..."

Breathing out a ragged breath, he took a moment to reply. Should he tell her that it had been unbearable? That he had changed his mind? Was that the truth or just a remnant of the hurt talking, pleading to be taken away, to return to his former self? He knew what had been done could never be undone.

He had chosen this. Chosen of his own human free will.

Being truly honest with himself as he contemplated how best to reply, he remembered he had been enthralled by her. That, from the minute he had unclothed her and revealed the truth of her, there had been no other thought in his mind but to join her. Be with her, and, if possible, be more like her. Then, love itself had infused their ribbons of blood, binding their destiny together, for what would now be an eternal lifetime.

"No longer Tarl, the smithy's son" he whispered as he

stroked her pale face. "Change is upon me." He pulled her closer again and searched her luminous blue eyes in wonder and forgiveness. She knew then that she had truly changed her destiny, the only future she now had was with him by her side. "And I, I relinquish Aioffe....she was alone and now is not," she said, with conviction and hope in her voice.

He could never know what it had cost her to change her intended future, for him, and for herself. She had no intention of telling anyone that 'fulfilling her duty and obedience' was no longer a part of her destiny. Those chains of responsibility fell silently from her shoulders as she took his hand and whispered earnestly, "Together, we can be truly free. But, we need to go now, before we are discovered!"

CHAPTER 2 - DISRUPTING DESTINY

September 1534

Tendrils of smoke filled the young man's sensitive nostrils with the scent of waxy paper, apples, sea salt and lichen-covered bark, evoking happier memories of the last five years. Shaking his long blond fringe away from his eyes, he poked the embers. Bright sparks gracefully leapt into the air and twinkled before vanishing with a quiet snap. He looked up at the clear skies overhead, the canopy of stars through the array of amber leaves blurring as his eyes welled up. Smoke caught in his throat. In it, he could taste the essence of their temporary home, and now was destined to change again. The thought of starting over again sat on his heart, heavy and full of dread and sorrow.

The snap of a branch behind him made him spin around, but his face quickly lifted into a smile as he saw her. Pale in the moonlight, her skin always glowed clearest at night, lighting the shadows with its luminescent tone. She smiled gently at him and held out a slim hand. "Ready?" she said softly.

"Soon," he answered, taking her chilled fingers in his and leading her to the warmed log at the fires' edge. Together in the still dark forest where they felt most comfortable, they sat silently by the bonfire as its embers dulled, slowly pushing in the papers nearer the core. They would leave no trace of their identities in this town - only taking their memories to remind them of what once was. The moment of sadness he felt earlier lifted in her company; she was, and always would be, his partner in their long journey to survive. Together they would carve out another future, in another town. It never got any easier, no matter how many times they resettled.

He replayed memories through his minds' eye as they destroyed all effects which could give their existence away and could be used by their pursuers. He recalled the lowered gazes from the once welcoming shop-keepers, a lull in conversation amongst the previously courteous ladies after church when they approached. Then, inevitably, the anger. Always under suspicion, they were ultimately people with no verifiable roots and who never quite fitted in.

Often, it started innocently enough with the women noticing something odd about the strangers. Talking, gossiping about why they weren't quite 'right'. Then the menfolk joined their wives, voicing their anger, their sense of injustice. Before long, something would happen which wasn't 'usual', and, having nothing more than guesswork and gossip to go on, sometimes the mob mentality started. The couple quickly became the target despite their efforts to lie low, especially if he or she had been tardy in spotting the subtle shift in attitude, or, like this time, stalling the inevitable so they might stay longer.

Here, the apples had tasted so juicy, the surroundings so beautiful, they had almost left it too late to pull away. Life had been unexpectedly rich and varied, with its travelling performers and community rituals celebrated with gusto and wine. A temperate southern climate made it harder to resist the temptation to feed from them, especially her - she was trickier to keep sated. The people in this seaside township were generally so happy and full of Lifeforce, it was hard to leave them, for some he counted as friends. Stranger still to not say goodbye or make their excuses for leaving this time, such a pleasant time it had given them for a longer than usual number of years.

The sunlight was just starting to pick through the forests when he heard the voices. Faintly at first, but then growing closer. Then, the crash of dogs bounding through the drying undergrowth. Picking their way nearer to their hideout, he knew they would have discovered the empty house by now and come looking for them in the nearby copse. Maybe even the bodies of their chosen animals, desiccated and hastily buried in the dead of night, had been found.

He rubbed her shoulders in his lap, gently whispering, "It's time, my love, we need to go now. They are close." She opened her eyes and sat up quickly, blinking in the pinkish light of dawn, her ears picking up on the sounds as they got closer. The dying embers of the fire would give their location away, and she hurried to pick up the heavy leather sacks she had brought with her earlier.

A large, shaggy-looking dog bounded into the clearing, and taking a stance glaring at them, started barking loudly in clipped notes. Too quickly it was joined by other canines, circling them and noisily declaring their presence to the men surely not far behind. They were trapped. He stepped forward towards one of the dogs, making to shoo it away, but the dog growled, digging in with its haunches and baring yellowed teeth in a snarl. Fetid breath puffed in the crisp dawn light, surrounding them with a foul-stenching net.

The hounds wouldn't advance on them, instinct warning them they were not the top hunter in this instance. But they wouldn't betray their masters and back away. They had found their quarry and reward awaited them. Their eyes fixed on the couple, unblinking. Hunter versus hunter. Beast versus beast.

"We will be seen if we leave from here," she murmured, barely audible to most ears over the noise of the barks and snarls. She hurriedly fixed the straps behind her, the bag altering her slim silhouette, making her look strangely unbalanced with a protruding pot-belly where it hung. He looked bulky, cumbersome with his front-strapped sack on.

"Probably, but it's a risk I think we need to take," he said, "I'm willing if you are?"

"Over 'ere!" Shouts, sounding close, followed by dull snapping branches as boots crashed their path through the undergrowth.

She nodded and pulled the bonnet from her head to free her hair. Her shimmering wings unfurled, the morning light bouncing off them as it streamed through the tree leaves. "Straight up!" he said as he bent his knees to lift off, his darker wings already freed and waving slowly.

They shot up through the canopy and into the bright sunlight. The fields shrinking below were dotted with sheep and horses, mottled green and brown hedgerows marking their boundaries. Small thatched dwellings laid low to the ground, their stone chimneys spouting thin wisps of smoke as early morning fires were stoked. Higher they flew, out of the range of the voices shouting louder now as the enraged and frightened group, bearing pitchforks and bows, found the still-warm ashes of the fire. Higher, to where the birds circled, swirling in formation in their morning gathering.

Looking up through the trees, one of the men saw their odd-shaped silhouettes, out of reach of arrows, disappearing into the clouds. Shaking his head, the notion that he had witnessed something not of his world was quickly forced out from his mind - it did no good to stir up further talk of the devil amongst them. A man would only have to spend yet more time in the confessional and at prayer if he had seen anything sinister, after all. Best not to mention it.

*****

"Who shall you be today, my love?" she called over the clouds. "I like the name Joshua!" He smiled and shook his head, grinning at her, "You like Joshua because you liked the boy, not because you like the name, I think."

"He had the sweetest tasting Lifeforce I have had in a long time," she said, remembering, "but I nearly got carried away. I caused this relocation and for that, I'm sorry."

"You are insatiable, in more ways than one," he called back, moving closer to grasp her hand mid-air. They slowed, joined hands then fluttered to face each other. In the brilliant sunlight, they gazed at each other, searching, studying and reconnecting. Together they hovered, hands clasped around the bulky sacks with their only belongings in, two sides of a lumpy, bejewelled butterfly. In the unfiltered light, high above the clouds, their love glowed through in its intensity. It would be absurd to think that they had ever blended in, no human would ever have mistaken them for being mortal had they seen them now. Fair skin, ash-white hair almost translucent as the sunshine poured through it, and wings rippled with rainbow tones fluttering as they wavered, lingering in the moment.

"I can't promise more boys like him," he said, looking now at her lips as he leaned in for a kiss. "And we must try to blend in more next town, and not risk losing control with a human, however much we get lost in their energy. We can survive without them, you know!" He reproached, but still with love in his tone. "We could have stayed longer if only we had been more careful. I think the lad will recover with some rest. The young usually do, then attribute their lack of get up and go to over-doing it or some sort of malady."

She smiled and nodded, but she still felt guilty. Her need for sustenance from the unseen joy humans emitted was addictive. The Lifeforce their kind gained from its root source in blood was enough for him, but satisfying her own needs was more dangerous and required crowds of humans. Keeping control of herself during these times was always a challenge. A moment or two longer in her thrall, and it would have been too late for that poor boy. She sometimes forgot herself in those heady inhalations, but had so far never broken her own rule of not killing a child in the heat of the inhale. But youth, they were so free, so deliciously innocent. Their Lifeforce had no filter and its purity was sublime.

"I just want to build a home with you, where we can be at peace. I don't think that's too much to ask?" Joshua's begging broke her guilt-laden reminiscing.

She pulled back from the embrace, and stroked his face, feeling the boyish stubble along his jawline. "I know, I need that too," she said wistfully. "Maybe this next time..."

"You always say that..."

"I know."

"Never satisfied," he teased.

He flapped his dark wings and spun her around and around, she leaned her head back and relaxed her back, allowing him to take the lead in a dizzying spin. They both laughed at the release of the exhilarating action. As he slowed, he lowered his face to embrace her again.

"My head!" she said, breaking off the kiss, "It's still spiny...if this is what death feels like, I could die right now, happy. It's like a little death."

"Believe me, this is not what dying feels like," he said, nuzzling her ear. "I could remind you what a 'little death' feels like if you want though?"

Her grin broadened, "You'll have to catch me first!" She darted upwards, playing. Like dancing dragonflies, they dashed around the skies, giggling and whirling.

"I won't lose you again minx!" He caught her slender ankle, "I will follow you, find you, hound you down like we are hunted now, even if there were an arrow still jutting from my side!" He paused, hovering up to look her fully in the face earnestly, lovingly.

Stroking the hair from his face, she whispered, "Never, I'll never truly run from you. Nothing will ever part us." They embraced again, and he gave her bottom a cheeky squeeze through her skirts before he pulled away. Squealing in mock outrage, she pushed away from him and dashed off. He followed, of course, and they continued their journey north together.

*****

They slowed after a few hours, and dipped down through the cloud cover, to where it was raining and grey. Flying lower yet still out of sight, looking for a group of houses - a town, not just a village. He pointed northeast, and together they gracefully swung around and headed for a small wooded area on the outskirts. Rough tracks could be seen weaving their brown trails around the countryside, fields less enclosed by hedge than their last location. Through the drizzle, the muted colours of leaves turning golden amber as the autumn set in provided sufficient cover for their landing.

They landed down by the side of the woods and adjusted their packs to cover the wings now tucked away behind their backs and under clothes. Helping each other, they straightened their attire, tidied hair into caps and tucked smock edges neatly into jerkin and kirtle. It all helped to ensure their windy and unusual travel method (and themselves) would not attract undue attention. Holding hands as they picked their way through the muddy tracks and avoiding the puddles left by carts and carriages, the young couple headed towards a cluster of buildings ahead.

"How about Annabella? For me. Mistress Annabella

Meadows," she said softly to him as they approached an Inn which sat on the crossroads of the road-track into town. It was getting dark and experience had taught them it was best to view a new possible home in daylight.

"I'm flattered you remember my little treats," he said with a smirk on his lips, "and a fitting way to honour her charms. I plan to demonstrate how stimulating I found her Lifeforce, just as soon as we find our next abode." Giggling, they pushed open the faded oak door and entered the Inn, hoping to find a room for the night where they could rest. The smell of damp leather and stale ale assaulted their noses as they crossed the threshold. But, there was comfort in the humanity within and a warm hearth.